Young Shoulders

Also by John Wain

Poetry
A Word Carved on a Sill
Weep Before God
Wildtrack
Poems 1949–1979
Feng

Fiction
Hurry on Down
Living in the Present
The Contenders
A Travelling Woman
Nuncle and Other Stories
Strike the Father Dead
The Young Visitors
Death of the Hind Legs and Other Stories
The Smaller Sky
A Winter in the Hills
The Life Guard
The Pardoner's Tale

Autobiography
Sprightly Running

Criticism
Preliminary Essays
Essays on Literature and Ideas
The Living World of Shakespeare
A House for the Truth
Professing Poetry

Biography
Samuel Johnson

John Wain has also edited
Johnson as Critic
Johnson on Johnson

Interpretations: Essays on Twelve English Poems
Selected Poems of Thomas Hardy
Personal Choice: A Poetry Anthology
Anthology of Modern Poetry
Anthology of Contemporary Poetry
Everyman's Book of English Verse

YOUNG SHOULDERS

John Wain

M

ISBN 0 333 34055 8

First published 1982 by
MACMILLAN LONDON LIMITED
London and Basingstoke
Associated companies in Auckland, Dallas, Delhi,
Dublin, Hong Kong, Johannesburg, Lagos, Manzini, Melbourne,
Nairobi, New York, Singapore, Tokyo,
Washington and Zaria

Printed and bound in Great Britain
at The Pitman Press, Bath

Graham's

In the early 1960s, a chartered airliner carrying a party of English schoolchildren crashed in, I think, Switzerland, with loss of life. I remember seeing a newspaper photograph of the rows of candles in the church where the requiem service was held, which the parents were flown out to attend. The story lay in my mind for twenty years and surfaced at a time when I was staying in Lisbon, with my friends Mike and Anne Eltenton. Since I was so immersed in the atmosphere of Lisbon and so familiar with its lay-out, it was natural for me to set the novel there; but I ought to say, in fairness, that as far as I know there has never been an accident of this kind at Lisbon Airport; nor, for that matter, have I ever personally known a parent who had lost a child under these circumstances. The story and the characters, though I hope true enough to life, are imaginary.

J.W.

Contents

One

Sitting on the back seat, looking between their two heads at the road coming towards us, I find myself wondering if I'll get a drive. Might as well try it on:

'Mind if I have a drive, Dad?'

At first I think he hasn't heard me, then he half turns his head in that soft check-pattern tweed cap he wears for travelling, and speaks, his voice quiet and a bit dreamy, as if he's away somewhere else in his thoughts.

'We're nearly at the motorway, you can't drive there till you've taken your test.'

'I know that. I meant after we get off the motorway.'

'I'd rather you didn't. It's a complicated route to find and we daren't risk being late.'

'Well, I could drive and you could navigate.'

The other one suddenly snaps her head round and says to me, irritated:

'It doesn't matter whether you drive or not, Paul. You get plenty of driving practice without pestering for more of it at a time like this.'

Well, there it is. *At a time like this* no one should be thinking of anything else. *At a time like this* I ought to feel ashamed if I unzip my trousers and have a pee.

I dare say their sorrow *is* worse than mine, but the point is, I feel mine differently. They seem to think of sorrow as being like a thermostat, or like a tap that you can turn on and leave at a certain adjustment, either a slow trickle or a quick rushing stream. Go away and forget about it and the tap stays at that adjustment till you come back and change it. My grief isn't like that, it's more like a wind that blows through me and then dies away. But of course I don't try to explain. They've gone past the point where they can listen to one another, let alone to me.

Here's the intersection for the motorway. We slow down for a moment, get into the right lane and then Whoomph. I'll be glad when I get my hands on a car. Even the lessons aren't bad fun. One of the ways in which seventeen is *definitely* better than sixteen.

The motorway. Cold, soaked green fields rushing past. It's after Easter, Clare's trip was in her Easter holidays, but there's been so much cold rain, nothing looks very summery yet. Long streaks of flood-water in the fields. The hedges just turning green, nothing on the big trees yet. Clare hardly saw the beginning of this spring. That means she only saw twelve. This one would have been her thirteenth. What's it like when you've seen forty-five of them, like him, or forty-two, like her: d'you get blasé? Or is each one more precious as you get fewer and fewer ahead of you?

Off the motorway, down a tangle of streets with dry-cleaners and car accessory shops and betting offices. Signs begin to come up, WELCOME TO HEATHROW. The usual debate starts:

'Did they say Terminal Three?'

'No, surely One, wasn't it?'

'Ought to be written up somewhere, keep looking out.'

Christ, he's been on enough trips abroad, you'd think he could remember which terminal it is. Never lets go the chance of a trip. Needs to be away from home, I suppose.

We're here, this is the right terminal, this is the car-park, up and up storey after storey, climb, right-angle bend, climb, right-angle bend, then find a space, inch in, get out, take the cases out, lock the doors, goodbye old car till tomorrow afternoon. Listen to all those 'planes taking off and think internal-combustion thoughts. You could run the car for nine years on what it takes one of them to cross the Atlantic. All the different places you could visit in nine years, the people you could go to see.

She and he are sharing a suitcase, I'm glad they still share something. Mine's a little overnight bag, plastic, with ADIDAS written on it, like little kids take when they go on a day excursion to see a football match. I talked about seeing a nice lightweight suitcase in the department store, hint,

11

hint, no result. Well, I dare say money is tight. Whisky's God knows how much a bottle. Went up again last budget. Stick to plastic Adidas till I go to college and my student grant comes through, then perhaps I'll get my hands on a few decent belongings of my own.

Inside the terminal building and there's a man waiting for us by a blackboard. Yes, actually a blackboard with chalk. Seems funny they don't use something more modern and jet-age. An official of the airline company and he's had to chalk a board. IRONSTONE SCHOOL. PARENTS LISBON FLIGHT. INFORMATION HERE.

So Dad goes up to him and shows him the sheaf of tickets that came through the post and he bows his head forward a bit and looks grave and sympathetic and points out where we have to go. Through Gate Twelve to the departure lounge. Well, at least it isn't Gate Thirteen. Clare's was probably Thirteen. Is that a joke? Am I making a silly, frivolous little joke inside my head *at a time like this*? Not really. Fate isn't a joke, bad luck, superstition, fear, they aren't jokes. Unless, of course, everything's a joke, the universe is a joke, and God just one big hollow laugh.

We walk down the length of the concourse. Gate Thirteen, I mean Twelve. Passports, nothing else, everybody just waves us through when they see our tickets and realise that this is the Ironstone lot. And always with the same expression: we're sorry, we're a bit ashamed, we'd like to do everything we can for you.

Departure lounge. Rows of seats facing down the room towards the exit for the 'plane, other seats running round the walls. We sit on three along the wall. A stewardess is going round with a clip-board, checking names on a list. Mr and Mrs Waterford and Paul. Clare's parents and Clare's brother. Yes, that's us. Now take us to Lisbon.

We're sitting here like the Three Wise Monkeys. Hear-all, See-all, Say-nowt. Won't somebody give us something to look at? I didn't bring anything to read (at a time like this) though if I'd thought of it in time I might have brought *The Tibetan Book of the Dead* or something. Sorry, Clare. I'm really not trying to be funny. It's life, it's things in general, even death, that are being funny, not me.

Look round at the people we shall be with for the next twenty-four hours and a bit more. Everybody keeping their eyes down. Sorrowful faces, quiet voices, nobody actually making a *fuss*, nobody jumping up and down and screaming, We sent our kids up in an aeroplane and where are they? We want our kids back! WE WANT OUR KIDS BACK!

Hullo, though. There is one chap who looks as if he'd like to do something – bang his head against the wall, or bang someone else's head, or slam his fist through a plate-glass window. Tall, stringy, a youngish bloke, straggly fair hair and ditto ditto

13

moustache, mousy little wife beside him trying to keep him quiet. They don't quite look Ironstone material to me; not posh and well-bred enough. On the way up, perhaps, trying to give the kid a good chance, get his nose out in front. Wonder what it's like at Ironstone. Thank God the old man wasn't as far up the ladder when he had me, didn't get expensive ideas, left me in peace at the local school. Clare liked it all right, though. Anyway, him and the ladder, that's a laugh. He's just far enough up it not to have to call himself an out-and-out failure. Back to the stringy man. He can't sit still. He keeps crossing and uncrossing his legs, twisting his hands together. His eyes swivel about as if he can't keep them focussed.

Now a man's stood up and is speaking to us, an airline man, the same poor sod who stood by the blackboard. Flight arrangements. Plus the usual line in soothing talk. All very sorry. Share your feelings. Shall do everything we can to make your visit this and that. Rely on our complete co-operation.

I'm watching the chap who's got the jitters. Having a bet with myself, will he get through the speech without jumping and interrupting? Everybody else is too well-bred to look towards him, no, wait a minute, there is one bloke, sitting two or three places away, who's watching him as openly as I am. A short, podgy chap, legs only just long enough to reach the floor from his seat, doggy little moustache. He looks a bit what my grandma would call 'common'. (My parents aren't looking, of course. They're not common.)

The official wishes he could sit down. Only a few sentences more. He looks round as if hoping to be rescued. The headmaster should be here. Robert Fawkes, M.A., Cantab., the one who looks keenly out at you from the prospectus, the headmaster will be here, in a moment. He's been held up. By four masked men, I suppose. He's talking to the Press. Oh, so they are masked men.

As he says that about the Press, the podgy man with the little moustache gives a kind of – well, not a start exactly, not as much as that, but a sort of movement of the head as much as to say, I heard that. The official goes on. The two aircraft will come up to the embarkation point one after the other. There have to be two, because the school party was enough to fill one, and as most of the children had two parents and most of the parents have accepted the invitation to come along, well, one times two is two, he seems to be trying to get round to the point of conveying, when —

Yes, it's happened, the stringy man with the thin fair hair is on his feet, he's shouting, he's waving his arms about, his little wife is trying to hold on to one of his arms but she's getting nowhere, he has this high-pitched voice and they must be able to hear him all over the airport.

'Two 'planes, is it? Two for the price of one! I

15

hope they're better maintained than that junk-heap you sent our kids up in!'

Grab, grab. His wife's really trying to pull him down beside her, as if they were in bed and he was having a nightmare. But he keeps shouting on.

'If they aren't, you'll be having another memorial service and nobody to go to it except lawyers!'

What's going to happen now? He's finished shouting but he doesn't sit down, his voice seems to go echoing round and round in a whirlpool of silence, everybody's looking down at their shoes, only the airline official is looking at the man, trying to think of something to say. Even I'm not looking at him, though I can tell the doggy little man is, because I'm looking at him and that's the direction of his eyes; no, they've swivelled, he's looking at the entrance door, I look too, and yes! Help has arrived, the United States Cavalry, John Wayne, Burt Lancaster, it's all happening.

This strong-looking bloke, muscles that could only have come from rowing since in his social bracket they won't have come from coal-heaving, oh, I know the score, I may be only a sixth-former but I've got it all plotted, and why not, you've got to know the score if you're going to run an outfit like the World Free Zone, yes, yes, this must be the headmaster, Robert Fawkes, M.A., Cantab., that face in the prospectus that used to make me think, this chap's educating my sister, will any of his correct attitudes rub off on me, God forbid?

He's speaking now, Robert Fawkes, and he has his hands in the pocket of his well-cut jacket, he's wearing a suit, it must be his speech-day suit to give out the prizes, I bet he wears a blazer and flannels the rest of the time, the popular headmaster, rumpled clothes, short hair just going iron-grey but boyishly curly, all right I'm taking the piss but actually he looks quite a decent bloke.

The official shuts up and lets him talk. Even the stringy man is subsiding, slowly, into his seat. His wife keeps her hand moving up and down at his sleeve, the way you'd pat a horse's neck to stop it from shying.

'Ladies and gentlemen, excuse me for not being with you till now. In fact I've been at the airport for an hour, but I've been dealing with reporters. The media are all here, newspapers, television, radio. In a way it sickens me, and yet I realise it's a matter that people are legitimately interested in. They want to know what happened, they want to know what we all feel about it. But that's where I'm determined to protect you. I gave very careful instructions that they were to be kept away from you, and I'm glad to say those instructions were carried out. I've dealt with them myself, which is only right, because I'm the only person here who isn't suffering the shock of bereavement.'

Pause. He looks down. Digs his hands more deeply into his jacket pockets.

'And yet that isn't quite true either. I *am* suffering

17

bereavement, not as intimately as you are and yet very deeply, because I did love and care for all these children. What's more, I feel a particular pang because you'd given them into my charge.'

Another look down, then a sudden, challenging look up.

'At Ironstone we believe very strongly in taking the children about and showing them the world. We believe that school isn't just a matter of sitting in the classroom. A lot of the youngsters know a surprising amount about the world even before they come to us. As a boarding-school, we get the sons and daughters of people who work overseas; at the beginning and end of each term, they get on jet 'planes and go halfway round the world. And every time they do that they're at risk to some extent, because with any kind of transport, accidents will sometimes happen. All I can say is that we shall go on running these tours, which the children enjoy so much and get so much out of, and we shall continue to use air transport, including, no doubt, this very same airline that's flying us all out today.

'As for ... the accident, there is, as you know, an official enquiry going on. But whatever the enquiry finds, we all know that human error does exist, and so do unpredictable weather conditions and million-to-one chances generally. And now, a million-to-one chance has happened and has struck you with the dreadful grief and suffering that

18

you're going through now. Believe me, I understand. And I share your feelings as much as anyone can who didn't actually lose a child.'

Eyes down again for a minute as if thinking what to say next. A woman is quietly crying somewhere; I look round but I can't see who it is. I suppose Fawkes can, but he goes on anyway.

'As a matter of fact, the only reason I'm standing here talking to you is because one million-to-one chance operated against another.'

? their faces say.

'This, as you know, was a tour of the Iberian peninsula. Mostly we were going to see Spain – Muslim Spain, in the south – but we thought it would be even richer if we started with a look at Portugal. So we arranged a few days in Lisbon and then on to Madrid. And, as you know, the accident happened as the 'plane was taking off to fly from Lisbon to Madrid.

'I wasn't on it, only because some administrative problems had cropped up at the last minute, as they often do in a headmaster's life, and I had to carve a few days off the beginning of the trip. So I arranged to miss Lisbon and go straight to Madrid. That's the only reason I'm here. But there are two Ironstone staff, two fine young teachers, who aren't here because they were in that 'plane with your children. They were Peter Richardson and Eileen Whitaker. Many of you knew them. They were both very dedicated, they were fond of the

19

children and they were with them to the end. Miss Whitaker's parents live in the North of England and I gather they're not in very good health, so they're understandably not with us on this journey. But Peter Richardson leaves a widow and she's with us today. Remember her sorrow as you bear your own, and let us try to help and strengthen one another.'

Where is this Mrs Richardson? I'm following his eyes. Oh yes, a tall, fair-haired young woman in a grey dress, sitting quiet, alone. She can't be more than, say, five years older than me. Well, seven or eight. Nothing in it. She could be one of the foundation members of the World Free Zone.

He's finished now, he's shutting up, and we're left to our thoughts while they sort out who's going to fly on what 'plane. Dad says he's going to the men's room and I ought to do the same. Sod that. Let him keep his advice. I'll go on the 'plane. He gets up and goes, and while he's away, maybe three minutes, I watch my mother. Here we go. Out comes the flask, she unscrews the top and takes a long, long swig. Whisky? Brandy? Never mind, whichever it is she needs it, and the top goes back on the flask and the flask disappears into her bag, and now he's back, fresher, more alert, bladder emptied, and I'm left wondering why she bothers to wait till his back's turned, why she doesn't just get the flask out and belt away at it right there before his eyes, as a way of saying to him *This is what you've reduced me to, you bastard, with your spinelessness and your depressions and your furtive little bits on the side,* but I hardly have time to think about it because the stewardess is making an announcement, it's time to stand up, it's time to move along in a queue, it's time to go to Lisbon.

First report to Clare

We're climbing up, up, up, raked back at a steep angle, piercing the sky, and all of a sudden I'm talking to somebody and it's you, Clare. Yes, by God, it's you.

Why is that such a surprise? Aren't you the reason we're all here anyway, so what more natural than that you should be in our thoughts, mine and everybody's?

Yes, but *talking* to you. Because that's quite clearly what I'm doing. I can feel that you're somewhere quite close to me and you're listening. That's pretty much of a novelty by itself. Listening isn't one of the things you went in for much, in your short life – but wait a minute, I can't start talking about your life as if it was over, all a thing of the past, you *did* this and you *were* that, because you're obviously still around.

Oh, come on. I'm imagining things. I suppose all this upheaval has been playing hell with my nerves, not that I've noticed anything special, and then perhaps altitude changes people's perceptions, like a drug. I'm rising from the earth at x feet per second and so I'm imagining things, hallucinating a conversation with my thirteen-year-old sister who's no longer alive.

Ow. That hurt. It was just as if you'd kicked me, on the shin or the ankle or somewhere. I can't say exactly where, because I didn't exactly feel it with my body, I felt it with my mind. But you did something, didn't you, Clare? You kicked or prodded or tweaked me somehow, to say *stop pretending I'm not here*. OK, OK, you're here. Don't do it again, that's all.

The NO SMOKING FASTEN SEAT BELTS signs are going out. We're at our cruising height. I can feel in my body that we've levelled out. And you're still here, aren't you? Close to me somewhere. Waiting for me to talk to you. And that's what I want to do, though I must say it's pretty funny. Funny that I want to, I mean. I didn't bother to do much talking to you when you were actually around, in your normal shape. I liked you all right, and it was quite fun having you about the place – mostly – but I never thought you'd understand much if I tried to explain anything to you, anything that I was thinking. Now, yes. Now, I feel you *would* understand. What's happened, Clare? Have you changed, or have I?

Perhaps it's you. Yes, I really think that could be. This ... whatever it is that's happened to you, I don't think you'd let me call it death, I really think it might have put you in a position to see and understand all sorts of things. I know I want to talk to you, and I know I have absolutely no need to talk *down* to you, as a grown-up to a kid.

Well, an *almost* grown-up. I feel pretty grown up, actually. I don't suppose there are any really big changes to come. I mean, I've changed a lot since I was your age ... I mean, the age you *were* when you ... oh, let it go, you know what I mean.

Look, what I'm trying to say is that I feel we can start fair. When we talk, I don't have to give you any briefing or background or New-Readers-Start-Here.

I'm quite sure, for instance, though it's no good asking me *why* I'm sure, that you know, now, just how things are between Mother and Dad.

You know, I often wonder whether their sending you to Ironstone was anything to do with that – whether they thought if you were away at school and only came home for the holidays, they could put off the day when you saw how things really were. A little kid just *accepts* everything – you don't realise that your parents are any different from other people's because you don't know what grown-ups are *supposed* to be like.

Come to that, I can't remember the exact *moment* when it dawned on me. I mean, there wasn't one morning when I woke up and said to myself, 'My father and mother have just about given up trying to make a relationship, he neglects her and she drinks.' Till I was about fourteen, I was young enough to see it simply from my own point of view – what *I* was going to get as my share of their help

24

and attention. If it had been one of those nights when I lay awake listening to them quarrel, in what they thought of as low voices but were perfectly loud enough for me to hear every word, I'd think, 'Well, at least she'll be up to give me my breakfast.' If I hadn't heard them quarrelling, that would have been because she'd gone to bed an hour or two before he did and drunk herself blotto. The night would be peaceful then, but on the other hand she'd have a hangover and I'd have to wake myself up and find the right clothes and get some breakfast, with such help as the old man could give which amounted to nil. He wouldn't have a hangover but he'd have black depression. It hung about in clouds all over the house, and before you went to Ironstone, when you were just at primary school, it always used to amaze me how you never seemed to notice any of it. Just took everything at face value. If Mother had gone to bed early, while you were still up and I was doing homework, well, she'd gone to bed early, why not? And yet it was perfectly obvious to a grown-up or even to an older kid, that she'd collapsed into bed at eight o'clock because she'd been steadily soaking up whisky since about lunch-time.

Poor Mother. I think she must have had high hopes once. That stage career that never started. She must have been good-looking, she still is in a kind of worn-out way, and of course with being tall, and carrying herself well, she had what they

call Presence. That's what our English master at
school said to me once, after they'd come to a
parents' evening or something. 'Your mother has
Presence, Waterford.' I remember thinking Yes,
and she has Absence, too, when she's been at the
bottle.

I'm sorry for them, Clare, of course I'm sorry for
them, but I can't afford to let myself be sucked
down into a kind of marsh of sympathetic misery. I
mean, I could easily brood about it all, I could get
self-pitying about what a handicap it is for me to
have to grow up in a household with an unhappy
relationship between my parents, seeping into
everything and turning it sour and putrid. Or I
could start yearning over the two of them, thinking
what a waste of their lives. You can consume a lot
of energy like that – just pouring it away in useless
regret, feeling sorry about things you can't alter.
But not me. I can't afford to do it, Clare. I need my
energy and I need to keep my head above the tide
of all this misery and bickering, because my life has
a Purpose. When I get a chance to talk to you for a
bit longer, I'm going to tell you what it is. I'm sure
you'll be interested. And it'll be marvellous to talk
it out to you, now that you're so ... so ... well,
you know what I mean.

I won't start on it now, though, because I think
I'm going to be interrupted. There's a stewardess
coming round with coffee or something. And the
old man's showing signs of wanting to Make

Conversation. You know that rather dog-like look that comes into his eyes when he's afraid of being rejected. Heck, I'm going to keep clear of the awful morass of his emotional life but that doesn't mean I'm going to be cruel to him. We'll talk later. Get ready to hear something really interesting.

Two

I haven't got a watch but I enquire the time and suddenly we're within half an hour of arrival. I go along to the lavatory while the going's good. Walking down the length of the aircraft I pick out people I'm beginning to recognise. Fawkes is sitting with Mrs Richardson, they're talking quietly and seriously. The stringy man who made the disturbance is staring out of the window; he looks angry, he's looking at the wing as if willing it to fall off and prove him right. The man with the doggy little moustache is having a big whisky and soda. On the way back, approaching him from behind, I can see the roll of fat bulging over his collar.

Now we're beginning to bump, the signs go on, we're sloping down and those roads and cars and houses down there are Portuguese roads and cars and houses, with Portuguese people in them. What is it like to be them? Is it any different from being me and growing up in a quiet, respectable market town in Berkshire, going to the local secondary school, dead centre middle-class, father an architect, not a success in his profession but not a total failure either, just a quiet sea of boredom all round – is life any less boring if you're foreign, say Portuguese or Spanish? It's supposed to be good for people to travel and see other countries, Clare's school was starting her on that already at thirteen, but then it's a posh school. I'm glad I don't go there. Might as well be bored at home as be bored at school twenty-four hours a day. I've been to France, that seemed all right. Must keep an open mind and suss out all these countries; one of them might turn out just right for the World Free Zone.

We're almost down now, the runway under our wheels a grey flowing carpet, then bump, bump, and a smooth slowing and rolling to a halt. At once the sun feels warm through the windows, giving the whole interior of the 'plane a holiday feeling. It isn't a holiday, of course, we're here to say we're sorry about Clare and the other children, but Clare won't mind, she'll understand. She wouldn't want me to feel miserable for the sake of feeling miserable. She was a kid who always liked cheerfulness; when she was little, if anybody had a long face she used to poke at them with her finger and say, 'Look happy.' Besides I know she's somewhere about, sharing in all this with us, I've been talking to her on the flight and she's been listening.

The airport terminal, the bus, we're off, this is Lisbon. A long straight main road with the sea on one side, big blocks of flats, garages, things like that. Palm trees. Now we're getting into town, the traffic's thickening. We run down into a kind of valley and up the other side. At the bottom of the valley there's a patch of waste ground, but no, it's

29

not quite waste ground, there are people living on it. They seem to be living in shacks, mostly, covered with tar-paper or something like that. They've got bits of washing hanging up. Very poor people. Are they hungry? Are people hungry here? I don't know anything about it.

We're here, this is our hotel. There are too many of us to be all in one hotel so we're parcelled out. I notice who's at ours. The doggy little man, the stringy man, some other odds and sods I haven't had time to notice. A couple of middle-aged people who look very like one another, as if they've lived together for years and always agreed with each other about everything, and eaten the same food and breathed the same air till they've become male and female versions of the same person. They walk just the same – very deliberate, very straight-ahead. They both have sandy hair.

The manager's fussing about. Finally everyone gets a key. I'm on the same floor as Them, but their bedroom's about halfway down the corridor and mine's right at the end, a poky little room but I don't mind, it's good to be by myself. I drop my bag down and go across to the window and get my head out. Hello, Lisbon.

The hotel's on a big main road. Very wide, with three lanes of traffic going each way, and then tram-lines with long yellow trams going along them like caterpillars, and then pavements with people walking. Eight lanes of traffic and two lanes

30

of moving people, ten in all, what a scene. I swivel round. Over to the right there's a railway bridge. As I look, a train draws slowly across the bridge, and a 'plane climbs the sky from the airport we've just come from. Suddenly it's like one of those posters they put up on the wall in language teaching, where you have to bring in as many objects as possible so as to use their names. FORMS OF TRANSPORT. The car. The lorry. The bus. The tram. The train. The aeroplane.

On the wall by the railway bridge someone's written in aerosol, so large that I can easily read it from here:

EM FRENTE PELO SEMANA DAS 48 HORAS!
EM FRENTE PELO CONTROLO OPERANO!
VIVA A ALIANCA OPERANO-CAMPONERA!

Wonder what all that means. I suppose I'll never know. There won't be time to learn any Portuguese in twenty-four hours. I've got a phrase-book, that someone at school lent me, but I doubt if I'll even get much chance to use that.

A tap on the door. It's the old man coming to brief me: the memorial service will be held at the English Church at six o'clock and we're to be ready to go at five-thirty. Meanwile, the time's our own. Lunch is ready downstairs, am I coming?

I say yes and we go back along the corridor. He goes into their room and I hear him ask if she's ready to come down to lunch. She says to go down and she'll follow us. He still hangs about and suggests we wait for her and all go down together. She says, 'Oh, do go *down!*' with an edge of impatience in her voice, and he comes out, pulling the door shut behind him. He looks tired, and papery and old. I know I ought to feel sorry for him, but I can't. I can't feel sorry for either of them. If they're making each other miserable, why don't they stop it? Treat each other differently, re-think the whole thing, or just split up and stop messing *my* life about.

In the dining-room downstairs, they've put a long table across the middle of the room for our party. People are coming in, couple by couple – the tubby bloke seems to be the only one who's here on his own – and it seems to be the done thing to take the next vacant seat on whichever side of the table you sit at. Very English. They don't leave empty spaces, they sit down next to whoever's there, but having done that they can't bring themselves to start a conversation straight away, they sniff round one another, and then of course there's that funeral atmosphere they've all got to keep up. Mustn't seem jolly. Even if you get absent-minded and forget your grief for a moment, you mustn't *look* as if you've forgotten it.

We sit down, me first, next to some nondescript people. A waiter brings food and I get stuck into it straight away. I'm going to cut this short and get out.

I took the first vacant seat, Dad took the second. Now the look-alike couple come in, pad pad, walking in that deliberate way, I'm sure they do everything in a deliberate way. They're younger than I thought at first; I wondered if they were the grandparents of one of the kids, but they must be the parents, it's just that they're the kind of people who *act* old. They sit down, the woman first, and naturally she takes the seat next to Dad. This throws him because he's trying to hold it for Mother, so he gobbles something in his shy way.

'Er . . . I wondered . . . my wife . . . down in a minute, I just thought I'd keep . . .'

'Of course, of course.'

They both give those restrained little smiles and murmur something. They've got soft Scotch voices. We've got a master at school who talks like that. Very Edinburgh.

'Our name is Finlayson, Robert and Janet Finlayson.'

'Oh.' (Fidget, fidget, desperate glance round to me.) 'I'm Ben Waterford and this is our son Paul.'

They smile at me in a How-d'you-do sort of way and the man says, 'Good afternoon, Paul. Are you at Ironstone too?'

I don't want to be bothered with him so I say, a bit rudely I suppose: 'Hardly. I wouldn't be here if I'd been at Ironstone, would I?'

'You might,' the woman says. 'Not every member of the school went on that trip.'

33

Then she turns to Dad and says: 'Tell me, Mr
Waterford, was your . . . child a boy or a girl?'

'A girl. Clare.'

'So was ours,' she says, nodding and looking
sad. 'I wonder if your daughter ever mentioned
her? Juliet Finlayson?'

He looks blank. I suddenly hear my own voice
saying:

'I remember that name. Clare talked about Juliet
Finlayson to me. Said they were friends.'

It's a lie actually. I never heard Clare mention
that kid's name. Why did I say it? Then, when I see
the two of them looking a bit happier for a moment,
smiling, I realise why. It was to help them, because
I was a little bit sorry about having been rude and
shut the woman up.

More people have been coming in. Dad's
beginning to get dead worried about Mother. Does
she mean to come down to lunch at all? Or is she up
there, drinking herself stupid? He keeps twitching
and looking round towards the door. Then
somebody on the left of the Finlaysons passes a
carafe of red wine along. It stands in front of them
and they both look at it with the same pained little
smile that says, 'Drinking? At a time like this?' and
move it gently along, handling it as if even to touch
the glass was a bit much. It's in front of Dad now.
He looks at it longingly, hesitates, then moves it
along in front of me. I let it stay. I know what he's
doing – trying to set Mother a good example. If he

34

has none, perhaps she'll have none. It's up to me to pass it along but I don't, I let it stand there. I'm not joining in these little games. The people on my right don't need it, they've got a carafe of their own, and it can stay where it is for me.

Here's Mother coming in at last. She's not just coming in, she's Making an Entrance. I think, as I usually do when I see her among other and more ordinary people, what a striking woman she is. Yes, striking, that's the word for her. I think, as she comes across to us and sits down, for the millionth time, that I can easily see why it was that she had ideas once about going on the stage. Marriage finished all that. Marriage, and Kenningbury, Berks, and boredom, and a second-rate life, and kids, and the bottle. It's all written in her face. She sits down. Dad introduces the look-alike Finlaysons and they make a few polite noises. She switches on a smile, turns it towards them to dazzle them, then looks down at her plate and switches it off again. Then she sees the carafe of wine, reaches out and gets her hand round the neck of it. Gurgle, gurgle, a good big glass. Drinks about half of it at a swig, fills the glass up again, and only then releases her grip on the carafe. Dad looks at it ruefully, standing there on the table in front of her, and then he takes it and pours himself a glass too. No point in trying to set an example any more. Ought I to have passed it along? Put it out of her reach? Of course not, she'd only have asked the waiter to

bring some, and in any case it's not my business
and I'm not interested. If my mother is an alcoholic,
that still leaves me with my life to live and I'm
going to live it.

I've finished my lunch. I ate too quickly and it
feels as if it's all stuck about halfway down, but I
can't help that. I take a swig of water to wash it
down, push my chair back and get up. I can see
Dad trying to catch my eye, but I won't have it
caught. Five-thirty back here, and in the meantime
I'm going to get away, be on my own for a bit.

But I have to go up to my room first, to get the
phrase-book, and then I can't resist taking a look
out of the window again, and then I mess about a
bit more, unpacking and hanging stuff up, and
they must have finished very quickly and come up
too, because as I go past their door I suddenly hear
their voices. Arguing, of course. God, how it takes
me back. All those nights when I've lain awake,
listening to them tearing each other to pieces in
these very quiet voices. In the end she usually
raised her voice and started yelling at him and to
hell with whoever was listening, but he never did,
he never raised his voice, kept on asking her to
keep her voice down and not wake the children. Or
if Clare was away at school and there was only me
at home he'd say, 'Don't wake Paul.' What a laugh,
don't wake Paul, as if anybody could sleep through
that. It wasn't just the noise, it was the vibrations of
strife, strife, strife that would have woken the dead

even if they'd never said a word.

And now they're at it again, here in Lisbon. I stop and listen for a minute and he's saying:

'I'm telling you quite simply that if you get drunk and can't get on to your feet and go to our daughter's requiem service you'll never let me hear the last of it.'

'Let *you* hear? Why should you come into it at all?'

'Because it will be my fault, for the very simple reason that everything that goes wrong is my fault and always has been.'

Then she starts raising her voice and they must be able to hear her in the next room.

'Oh, don't talk bloody nonsense. Go away and leave me in peace and stop talking bloody nonsense.'

'It isn't nonsense to anyone who knows your character.'

'Never mind my character. Concentrate on your own faults and leave me alone.'

I've heard enough, I'm afraid he might come out and then I'll be stuck with his company, so I leg it along the corridor, down the stairs and out into the street.

I'm going to walk by instinct. It doesn't matter where I go, it's all interesting and new and foreign and strange. This long main road with the ten lines of traffic – if I turn right I walk away out of town, so I'll turn left. All these heavy, solid buildings, big shops, big banks. One of red brick, sort of octagonal, a high wall, turrets topped with round globes, very fancy – I wonder what that is.

The people are all thinking foreign thoughts. They look quite nice, though. I wouldn't say they were very good-looking, no more so than most people at home. There's one who's really beautiful, though, just going by, that girl with big dark eyes holding herself very straight, tawny hair drawn back, she's a knock-out. There doesn't seem to be any middle range, though. They're either knock-outs or they're rather ordinary: stocky, with potato faces.

A big square with splendid shops and cafés. I have absolutely no money. With all the other things going on, it never occurred to me to bring any Portuguese money, and I haven't got a bank card or anything like that. I suppose Dad, in his vague way, dropped into the bank for some travellers' cheques or something, or perhaps he has a credit card that's valid here, but it wouldn't occur to him to focus on *me* for long enough to realise that I might need some walking-around money. Of course if I'd waited for *him* to finish lunch and gone for a walk with *him*, he could have staked us a cup of coffee or something, I wouldn't have needed money then. Perhaps he psychologically forgot to give me any money to try to keep me from going off by myself. It'd be just like him, and also just like him to do it at a sort of dreamy level, not quite bringing it into the light of his conscious mind, just 'forgetting to think about it'. That's his way of dealing with me, to forget to think about me, and something of the same kind from her too, except that the bottle does for her what absent-mindedness does for him. What a mess, what a bloody mess. And it's all, at bottom, because they're too busy fighting one another to have any energy left over for living.

Ah, well, no coffee for me, no sitting down at a nice café table and watching the world go by, I'll just walk on till I get to some quiet place where I can talk to Clare. On and on I march, a long straight main road, but now I realise it's driving towards the sea. A few more minutes and we'll be there, Clare and I.

Yes, here it is, a wide square, very stately buildings: looks like a big railway station over on the left, and beyond it a row of market stalls, no use to me, I can't buy anything. A statue of an important-looking man on a horse in the middle of the open space, his back to the sea and his face towards the city; another aerosol artist has written on the base of the statue: PARASITAS VAO TRABALHAR! I think even I can guess what that means. But you have to be careful who you start calling a parasite.

The sea straight in front, not exactly a harbour, just a jetty with a few boats moored to it, a low wall and a shingle beach.

Then, of course, I start picking up stones,

rummaging around for nice ones, I don't suppose I'll ever sit down on a shingle beach without doing that. It's pretty scungey gravel, the sea never gets to it, there are bits of old crabshell and sponge and man-made things too, broken plastic objects and beer-can rings and what-not. The thing I finally decide I like best is halfway between natural and man-made; it's a piece of brick that's obviously been in the sea for ages, perhaps years and years. It's brick, there's no doubt about that, made from a deep red clay, but in all that long soaking in sea-water it's changed its nature. It's become smoother, and also lighter, more biscuity. As if microscopic grains of salt have somehow got in among the grains of earth in the original clay, pushing them apart a little, making the brick ... well, porous would be putting it too strongly, but changing it into something lighter and gentler. Suddenly I know I must put it in my pocket to keep for ever, because it's my Clare-symbol.

Why that? Why is this piece of sea-salted brick a symbol of Clare?

Because it's changed into something different while staying the same. Immersion in the sea has done for it what immersion in death, or whatever the other dimension is called, has done for her.

And now in the warm spring afternoon, with the piece of brick in my pocket, Clare comes near to me in the quiet of this empty harbour wall. So let's get started.

Second report to Clare

Hello, Clare. I was just talking to myself about the change that's come over you. But you know that, you were near me when I picked up that piece of brick. I couldn't give the scientific reasons why this brick's different from when it was part of a building, and I couldn't find words for the change in you either, but I know it's there because talking to you feels so different now. When you were just my bubble-gum kid sister I'd never have talked to you about my most important thoughts, my plans and ideas, but now, well, it seems natural. That's one of the reasons why I got out so fast from the hotel, I needed to be somewhere quiet with you because there's really nobody on earth I'd rather talk it out to. That's funny because you're not really *on earth*, are you? But I suppose you are after all, because I don't believe there's a separate location called the Spirit World or anything like that, I think we're all in it together. You'll be there in the World Free Zone, when we get it going.

The World Free Zone, yes, that's what I'm going to tell you about.

Walk along the jetty, look down at the boats moored there. This one's a nice motor-launch, open cockpit up front, neat-looking cabin a couple of steps down, everything clean and shining with new paint. Somebody had a bit of money to spend. She's for weekends and fun, not a working boat. But I'd make her work. If I owned that boat, I'd get into her now, taking you with me, and start her up, and I'd go slowly along the coast, keeping an eye out for inlets, anything like a fjord or a creek, or perhaps the mouth of a river, and when I found something suitable I'd nose her inland, keeping a good look out on either side, and finally I'd moor at some point where there was a bit of peaceful green land, perhaps a few huts and cottages, nothing in the way of a town, but a human settlement, and I'd tie the boat up and go ashore and walk around. I'd talk to the people somehow, make them understand I wanted to get to know them and their land, and perhaps, if it looked right, I could make that the very first territory of the World Free Zone.

You're the first person I've told about it, Clare. That's not because it isn't all thought out. It's all blue-printed and ready. But I know people. If somebody under about twenty-five comes out with an idea, they don't bother to listen because he's bound to be too young to know anything. So I shall just keep it to myself, and mature it and perfect all the details, till I'm ready to launch it.

You see, I'm working pretty steadily at school, and the object is to get to college and do a professional training, it hardly matters what as long as it's for some kind of work that's reasonably useful, something that people want, and decently paid. I'll get a job doing something that'll get me to meet people, and mix with them and pick out the ones I can trust, and then when I'm about thirty I'll get together my nucleus, it needn't be more than a couple of dozen at first, though any number up to about a hundred would be useful, and we'll launch the World Free Zone. It'll be a neutral area that won't belong to any country and the people who live there will be free to develop as human beings.

They won't have any chains on them, you see, Clare. There'll be no private property, so nobody'll be working like a mule to try to get rich or keep up with the neighbours. And there won't be any marriage, people will just live together if they want to, and if they decide they don't want to any more, well, they'll just move apart. There won't be all that God-awful family life that we've had to go through, children'll be looked after communally. When you come to think about it, that won't be much of a change; after all, when they sent you to Ironstone what was that but getting you looked after by a set of professionals who they thought could do it better than they could? It was certainly true, too, by that time.

The way I look at it, Clare, is that in the World Free Zone nobody will live the sort of life that Mother and Dad live, making each other unhappy and spreading that unhappiness all through the house they live in, and that they sweat blood to keep up, and then everybody who lives in the house with them has to share that unhappiness, has to breathe it in all the time whether they want to or not ... I know that's how the idea of the W.F.Z. came to me in the first place. It's come on a long way since then, mind you, as I've seen the possibilities.

I'm still thinking over what seem to me the two most tricky points: where we're going to be located, and who's going to have authority. Actually I think they'll both solve themselves, when the time comes. We'll start in a fairly restricted area – five or ten miles square, that kind of thing – and we'll acquire the land by buying it. That's why a pretty poor country, like Portugal, might be best to start in. Once we're settled and people get to know about us, we'll get contributions from interested people all over the world, and we'll open other centres. One day we'll link them up, that'll be the real Zone, but I think that's a long way in the future. I might not even live to see it. Now about authority. I shall be the Founder, just because I had the idea, but I shan't be the Leader because there won't be one. Nobody's going to boss anybody around. People who want to come and join us will have a three-month trial period before they become citizens of the World Free Zone, but I don't think we'll have any problem getting rid of them if they aren't the type. I mean, we shan't need any police or frontier guards or anything like that because if they don't like it they'll just melt away. And we shan't need to guard ourselves against theft because with no property there won't be anything to steal.

So you see, Clare, I've got a lot to think about. I have to travel when I get a chance, and keep my eyes open for suitable places. When you were doing your Iberian peninsula trip with the school, I thought when you got back I'd try to find out from you what it was all like: not telling you what I wanted to know for, because you wouldn't have understood, you were just a kid. Not like now.

Three

Back at the hotel in plenty of time, clean up, get a tie on, then hang about downstairs. People are beginning to assemble. I'm getting to recognise them now, husbands and wives whose names I shall never know, they'll just stay in my memory as grievers, sorrowers: one man completely egg-bald, another very tall thin couple like long sad birds, and another pair who look like school children themselves, so young it's hard to believe they had a child of thirteen or fourteen.

Now they're all milling about, the bus will be here in a few minutes, and no sign of my lot. No, here's the old man, looking gloomy and worried. What the hell's happened now?

I ask him the only possible question.

'All ready?'

'Well, *I* am. And I think your mother'll be down. God knows I've told her enough times.'

I can see the situation. He's had a job to get her on her feet and start her dressing and putting her face on. He's exhausted and fed up and the only thought left in his mind must be, *Is it worth it?*

I don't know what to say so I don't say anything. If they're going to be like a pair of spoilt children at a time like this . . . there, now I'm doing it myself.

In the end, she makes it. The bus is here and most people are on it already, but she's not so far behind that it draws attention. And she's done a pretty good repair job. I suppose she had a good few drinks and slept heavily, but it doesn't seem to have done her much harm. Her face is a bit puffy, but she's standing straight and holding her head up and everything about her is very correct, a fine figure of a bereaved mother, she's not going to let Clare down.

The English Church in Lisbon: a wide main road, traffic swooping fast downhill, and the graveyard quiet inside its wall. The coach stops and we go through the gate, a peaceful green place, welcoming, a bit overgrown, friendly, not fiercely trimmed and not with headstones in straight rows. If the World Free Zone has graveyards, I want them to be like this.

We file into the church, ushers and people showing us where to go. When we get to our pew I go in first, Dad next, Mother nearest the aisle, exactly as on the aircraft. We all go straight down on our knees. I know this is the standard drill, but I'm watching out of the corner of my eye so that I can get up, and sit or stand, when everybody else does. We don't go to church often enough to have it all off pat. In fact I don't remember ever being in church with both my parents at once. Mother has fits of going to Sunday morning service and sometimes she likes me to come along. If Dad ever goes he does it by himself. People are stirring, getting off their knees; I get off mine.

Hold on though, I do remember one time when we were all in church together. I can remember Clare's christening. I was only four at the time, so it must be about my earliest memory, but I can see both of them standing beside a thing that I remember as being like a drinking-fountain: the font, I suppose. I can remember what they had on. Dad had a grey suit and he was standing there awkwardly, all legs and arms. Mother was holding the little tightly wrapped bundle they'd brought there to be named Clare. There were some dim aunts and uncles there, but I don't remember them. I can see Mother very clearly. She had on a black skirt and a black jacket and a very white blouse, frilly down the front, I think, and that dark red hair of hers looked very dramatic, and she was holding the little bundle very close to her. I don't remember anything about what happened except the bit where the vicar sprinkled some holy water on Clare's little red forehead. I didn't know it was holy water, of course, it was just water to me, and he sprinkled it and she yowled. I thought that was funny and I think I must have giggled, because I remember people looking down at me and shushing.

Mother's still on her knees, face hidden in her

hands. Are there tears? I can't see through her fingers. But I know what she wants most in the world. I know what she'd pray for if she thought there was a God who granted wishes like a magician in a story-book. She'd ask to be back on that day over thirteen years ago, standing by the font holding baby Clare in her arms. She'd like the last dozen years to be wiped away and go back before it all started going sour, back before Dad neglected her, before she started drinking, while she still had children who were children and a marriage that was a marriage.

Now they're off, it's the service, this is what we came for. There's a parson who's obviously the anchor man here, and another who it seems came out with us. I didn't notice him on the way out. I think he's one of the kind who won't wear his dog-collar until he absolutely has to, in church. The two of them start belting it out. I sit here, or stand, or kneel, when everybody else does, and I'm trying to feel the right things, but I can't, my mind keeps sliding off the subject. If Clare were here she could help me, but she isn't. She stayed outside, I think. If I could get out of this building and walk about in the graveyard under the old trees, and poke into the little overgrown corners by the half-sunk tombstones, I'd pretty soon run into Clare and we could be together and feel something about the dead children and the sorrow that's lying about everywhere in heaps. But I can't get out, I have to stay here till they've finished.

There's a great big table covered with a purple cloth set up in the nave or whatever it's called, and on it are rows and rows of candles burning away. I see now, they're for the children, a candle for each little snuffed-out life. I pick out one and tell myself it's for Clare, that's Clare's candle, and I fix my eyes on its tall steady flame, sending heat upwards and light out in a circle all round. But I can't attach any special Clare-meaning to it, it's just a candle, it ought to be helping prayers to rise up but I can't see that it is. The light spreads round, the heat goes up into the ceiling of the church, but the prayers are just lost in emptiness.

One of the parsons is reading something out:

'Behold, I show you a mystery: we shall not all sleep, but we shall all be changed, in a moment, in the twinkling of an eye, at the last trumpet: for the trumpet shall sound, and the dead shall be raised incorruptible, and we shall be changed.'

I like it, I like the words, the way they flow through my mind, they're like a wave of salt water pushing up a tidal river, driving the muddy river water back the way it came for a little while, holding off all the dirt and the plastic containers and orange-peel and fag-ends that the river's trying to spew into the sea. I like it though I've no idea what it's supposed to mean. And yet I do know, because Clare's changed, I knew her before and I know her now, and she's changed, though from exactly what is more than I can tell.

Mother hasn't got off her knees at all, she's just stayed there with her face hidden, wanting Clare back, wanting me back as a little boy, wanting Dad back, wanting to be standing by that font of thirteen years ago. She's not going to uncover her face or get up from her knees, and now they've nearly finished, a bit more praying, a hymn, the candles shining up into the dark timbers of the church ceiling, and now it really is over. People are standing up, or sitting down in the pews and making vague scrabbling movements to locate and gather up their belongings, and the organ's playing something different, something of a walk-out kind, and we're all moving into the aisle ready for off, when WHOOSH! over goes Mrs Richardson, tall young-womanly shape, grey clothes, down, down, from the vertical to the horizontal, not quickly, just crumpling and lowering herself down. She bends over, she takes hold of the end of a pew, she folds her knees, she goes down as deliberately as a camel, putting her hands on the cold tiles of the floor, getting her head down just at the second when she blacks out altogether. It's a faint in slow motion, an attack of giddiness and a black-out, it must be like a heavy theatre-curtain coming down between her and the world. Most people are too surprised to do anything but stand rooted to the spot and watch her, but Fawkes is there, he's been standing next to her, at once he's bending over her, helping her up, his hand under one armpit. Now he's got her sitting in a pew, bending forward, he's supporting her, she's lifting her head up, trying to open her eyes as the blackness clears away.

Now there's a bit of after-fuss, people moving towards them. 'Can I help?' 'I'm a doctor.' 'She'll be all right, I think, just passed out for a moment.' 'All very understandable. A difficult time, stress . . .' Blah blah. Dad and I walk on. Mother, finally rising from her knees, comes on behind, looking straight in front of her. It's impossible to tell whether she even took in Mrs Richardson's fainting-fit.

I'm outside, it's a spring evening and every-thing's charged, electric, the greens are very green and the trunks of the trees are very grey; I don't think I ever noticed grey as a real colour till now. Mrs Richardson falling down in the church, her grey dress made a picture with her yellow hair. And here's Clare, as I round the corner of a big old monument, I don't see her but I *feel* her. She's been outside while we were going through all the prayers and stuff, out here playing and poking around. You were always good at being by yourself, weren't you, Clare, you could be happy for hours with a ball, or with a bucket and spade when you were little. Thanks for being here, and Clare – I haven't much time now, we'll talk when I can get away from this crowd, later in the evening, but there's one thing I want to ask you now – you will come home, won't you? I mean, you will be in England with us – you won't only exist in Portugal because Portugal's where you were ... funny, I can't say 'You were killed,' that's because I don't believe it. You weren't *killed* just because you stopped existing in one way and started up in another.

They're still coming out, I've had all those thoughts and yet I've only been out here a couple of minutes. Look at them, Clare. The two clergymen are standing at the door, ready to have a word and a handshake with anyone. The parents, they've all got their own way of responding to this or not responding. That Scotch couple with the long, very correct faces, they come out ducking their faces gently up and down, I can just imagine the kind of sad, correct thing they're saying in low polite voices. And yet, as I stand here watching, something funny's happening. The wife walks straight past the clergyman without looking at him and goes on in a straight line, as if she's sleep-walking. The husband stops to make some correct, expected remark to the parson, then he suddenly sees that the parson isn't attending to him but is looking after Mrs Finlayson, who's still sleep-walking dead ahead. She gets to a big old monument with urns and things, just like a wall blocking her path, and against this wall she stops, puts her hands flat against it and lays her cheek against the stone as if she's listening to someone inside it tapping out a message.

The husband hurries over to her, puts his hand
on her shoulder and starts saying something to her.
I can't go on watching, it seems wrong, indecent,
prying, and I turn and look away. When I next
look, they've gone, and the chap who made the
disturbance, the stringy bloke with the tired patient
little wife always apologising for him, is coming
out. He doesn't pause to speak to anyone, he
doesn't approve of parsons hanging round, paid to
say the right thing, paid to hush the whole thing up
and stop people like him protesting. He glares at
them as he goes by, and his wife follows on behind,
lifting her eyes to theirs with a little smile,
apologising for his glare. And there's Mother, she's
looking straight ahead of her, she ignores the two
parsons not out of rudeness but because she really
doesn't see them. I can tell she's holding herself
together so as not to break into sobs and tears, or
faint like Mrs Richardson. How well she carried
herself.

Well, here's the bus, everybody's climbing back
into it; do they feel any different from how they felt
when the same bus brought them over here from
their hotel not much more than an hour ago? Has
that hour changed anything? I suppose when they
look back on it all, they'll remember the requiem
service and think, Well, we did Our Best, we did
Everything We Could. Only of course there's

nothing they can do.

Are the other kids alive like Clare? I can't answer that one. They wouldn't be alive to me anyway, because I didn't know them.

I'm thinking these thoughts, holding on to one of the uprights in the bus, and we're all swaying along. It's one of those foreign buses, kind of open plan, designed for a lot of standing passengers and very few sitting. The thought comes to me that I've really got a lot taller in the last year or so, since I turned seventeen, because as I turn my head and look about, my eyes are on a level with the eyes of most of the grown-ups. The women certainly, and most of the men, though not the tall ones like Dad. Funny how being tall, he isn't at all imposing with it. That's because he's so lacking in confidence, always expecting to be in the wrong. I could write his obituary:

WATERFORD, BENJAMIN. Died yesterday at his home in Kenningbury, Berkshire, without ever having properly lived. An architect, started out well, showed promise during student years, somehow it never came to anything. His original ideas, though often short-listed and always received with respect, were never finally chosen for a big project, and in middle life he sank without much protest into a routine job working for the local authority, designing school kitchens and bus shelters and things like that. Unhappily married. Two children at first: one later. Destined to go down to history as father of the great creative force of modern times, Paul Waterford, founder of the World Free Zone.

I keep looking round me at the faces, tired and thoughtful for the most part. There's one man whose eyes are actually lower than mine, he's shorter, a grown-up who's not as tall as I am. It's the doggy little man. I'd notice him anyway at this moment, because his expression is different from anyone else's. While they're looking sad and thoughtful, he's looking, what shall I call it, *hungry*. His eyes are darting about everywhere as if he's looking for something. He wants human contact, he wants to be talked to. He's undone the top button of his shirt and loosened his tie, as much as to say, The formal part's over and done with, for God's sake relax.

If he wants to spread that mood he's got to work hard because everybody else is very quiet and broody. It's as if a tent had come down over them all, a thick green tent. I know why, I understand, it's because their children's death has now been made official. Somewhere in everybody's mind there was a little wisp of hope that it hadn't really happened, that it was a nightmare they were going to wake up from, but those rows of candles finished it. Now they know it's real, it's had the seal of the Church stamped on it, the official words of hope have become official words of despair.

Still, he's at it, glancing round trying to catch the eye of somebody, anybody, to start a conversation with. He catches mine and gives me a friendly grin, he's too far off to talk to me through the intervening heads and bodies, but his grin says, *I know you're there, hello.*

As soon as we get to the hotel he's off the bus like lightning, little polished black shoes patting across the pavement getting in among the first so that he can take up a position in the lobby and grab people as they go past.

I get off the bus and wait for my parents, then we go in together, and as I thought: the doggy man's waiting.

'Beautiful service, wasn't it, everything done and said just right, and now what d'you say we have a drink and try to . . .'

Try to what, he doesn't know, can't put it into words, but he needs company and needs to get back to the ordinary little pleasures of life after all that solemnity: needs it so much that he's going to *force* people to come and have a drink with him if he can't get them any other way.

My parents hesitate just long enough to be lost. Dad hesitates because he's a natural hesitater. Mother wouldn't think twice about walking past him, but the word 'drink' gets hold of her; she must have a supply up in her room, but perhaps it's running short, perhaps she needs to conserve it, and there won't be time to go shopping.

He jumps at this chance.

'The bar's just here, I thought it was time we got to know each other, my name's Gerald, Gerald Worplesdon [or some name like that], I don't think we met at any of the school functions.'

'Oh. Ben Waterford. My wife, Martha.'

He turns to me, I'm included too.

'And this young fellow?'

'Paul. Our son, Paul.'

'Fine, come on in.'

They're caught now but he's still looking round for a more plentiful supply of victims, he wants to be in a *crowd*. The Finlaysons come past, padding quietly, discreetly, and he's ready with —

'Would you care to join us in a drink?'

Mrs Finlayson gives a small, pained smile.

Mr Finlayson gives a small, pained smile.

It's obviously a smile they keep in a drawer with clean white handkerchiefs and neatly rolled ties. They take it out and wear it when somebody makes a lowering suggestion. It fits over both their faces at once, the one smile.

'A drink, no thank you.'

'I don't think so, thank you.'

It doesn't seem to bother him. He looks round at the rest of us, sharing the joke.

'You always get that type. Look at you as if you've admitted to being a child violator or something, if you just suggest they join you for a drink when think they ought to be pulling a long face. And all the time I bet they've got a bottle of Scotch at the back of the wardrobe.'

I glance across at Mother. She shows no sign of having heard him.

'Well, let's sit down. What'll it be?'

He looks round for a waiter, but there isn't one, so he goes up to the bar. And returns in a moment with some glad news.

'Everything's on the house. The airline's going to pick up the whole bill, including the bar. You just give your room number. Pretty nice of them. I must say they're doing what they can.'

He's looking pleased, Gerald. The flesh of his face was sagging a bit in the bus, but now it's become round again, it's completely round like a little sweaty football. He's *awful* and everybody thinks he's awful and deep down he must know it. Or does he? Do people like him know the impression they make on other people? It's a question I'll have to go into, because what if a person like that wanted to settle in the World Free Zone?

Oh, but he wouldn't.

Well, but he might.

He'd go away at the end of the three months.

I hope so. I just hope so.

My parents are looking desperate but as usual they're being desperate *alone*, and not together. If only they'd share it, they might see the funny side.

Mother's got a big whisky in front of her with chunks of ice. That'll hold her for a few minutes, but only a few.

Now Gerald's spotted the disturbance man and his depressed little wife, walking past the door. He's out of his chair and after them – he can move fast when there's something he wants.

In the moment or two that he's otherwise engaged, my parents exchange glances and she asks:

'Who is this man?'

'I don't know. I suppose he must be a parent.'

He means an ex-parent, so the thought depresses him even more and he stares into his drink. I'm sorry for him but Christ, he's so *wet*. Gerald comes back with the other two, talking fast to keep them from bolting.

'That's the way, sit down and relax a bit, have a drink, I think we've all earned it.'

The man looks about him with those wild eyes as if he can't quite understand what's happening to him, why he's in this room with these people, why he's sitting down, accepting this drink, but the woman seems glad enough. Everybody makes the normal noises, getting introduced, it turns out their name's Smithson. Gerald comes back with a vermouth for her and a large whisky for him.

'It's on the house. The airline is really trying to do the decent thing.'

That was a mistake, he shouldn't have mentioned the airline. Smithson's eyes pop out a bit more. They're china blue. They don't look like a human being's eyes, more like something you'd see in a cheap doll. He's glaring at his whisky as if he's discovered, just in time, a plot to poison him.

'The decent thing. That's hardly the way I'd put it. Throwing some money at us now that it's too late. The decent thing would have been to fly our kids safely.'

Gerald's waving a plump little hand. He wants to shut the man up and get back to having a nice cosy time.

'Look, old man, instead of chucking blame about, why don't you just accept that accidents sometimes happen?'

'Accidents don't happen. There's no such thing as an accident. When things go wrong it's because somebody's made a mistake.'

'And you'll feel better if that somebody's searched out and punished.'

'I didn't say that. I didn't say I'd feel better.'

'Well, if it doesn't make any difference to how you feel, why not leave it alone?'

Smithson's wife is looking frightened. She can see an outburst coming. She's a little dark woman with a sad, lopsided face. She glances across at my parents, more particularly at Mother, one woman asking another to help her. But what can anyone do?

Smithson's gripping the arms of his chair and

now he's really turning on Gerald.

'Anybody'd think you were in the pay of the airline, you're playing their game so perfectly.'

'Steady on, old man, no need to be insulting.'

'Don't you see, that's exactly how they want you to react. Sit back with a free drink in your hand and don't ask any awkward questions.'

'Look, old man, there's going to be a formal enquiry. Surely we can wait till —'

'An enquiry! I know those enquiries and so do you. A whitewash job. Get a few aeronautics people up on the stand to say it was all an unfortunate business and nobody could have foreseen it.'

He gets up. He hasn't touched his drink.

'I'm going up to the room, Millie.'

He's marching out, now he's gone. She begins to cry softly, crumpling in her chair. Millie Smithson, a loser's name if I ever heard one. Mother's trying to comfort her. It brings her out in a rash of words.

'It's awful, Mrs Waterford, it's just awful trying to live with him, I'd find it hard enough to bear even if he was a *help*. Tracy was our only one and the doctor doesn't think I'll be able to have any more.'

Poor old Gerald's looking blank, he didn't bargain for this. Mother's making soothing noises, but the best thing is just to let her talk.

'I knew it was a mistake for Howard to come on this trip, I knew he'd find no comfort in it and it'd only upset him all the more. Though I don't think he could be any more upset really. He hasn't slept, he hasn't slept a single night since he heard about . . .'

Inarticulate words into a handkerchief.

'There, dear, don't upset yourself. All we can do is just go on living.'

'If he shuts his eyes at all in the night it's just for a few minutes. He keeps getting up and walking about the room. They offered him some leave from his work but he said he'd rather go in and occupy himself. But that didn't work. He used to sit looking at the same sheet of figures all day long. He was under everybody's feet. In the end they asked him to stay away till he felt better. But if you ask me he's never going to feel better. If you ask me he's going mad. And I don't know what to do. It'd be hard enough to bear it even if he was being a help to me.'

'I know, I know. Come, dear, I'll help you up to your room.'

The two of them go out. Gerald doesn't know what to say next. He looks at me and then at Dad. But Dad won't meet his eye and suddenly he's on his feet.

'Well, I think I'd better . . .'

He doesn't even finish the sentence, he runs out like a rabbit. Poor old Gerald. His little social half-hour is really shot. He looks across at me with a hurt expression. I've finished my glass of lager and

63

I'm plotting an escape too, he can probably sense that. He speaks, seriously, as if it was a dying message.

'I think that when troubles and sorrows come into your life, the thing to do is to put a good face on them. What do you think?'

He seems to be waiting for some sort of answer, so I fidget and say:

'It isn't always possible, I suppose.'

'People who can't put a good face on their suffering,' he answers slowly, 'ought to stay at home and go to pieces where no one can see them. They oughtn't to move about among other people and pull them down to their level. That's what I think.'

He gets up.

'Excuse me, I've got a telephone call to make.'

So he leaves me sitting there. I suppose the telephone call was a polite excuse. It meant that he could be the one who left instead of the one who was left. I think he saved a bit of face there, and I'm glad for his sake.

Third report to Clare

Hello, kid. I knew I'd find you waiting for me up here. Thank God I've got a room to myself. Funny, how strongly I can *feel* that you're here. I can't see you – perhaps there's nothing to see? – but you're here all right.

I wonder how I'd feel if I didn't know that. If I thought that you'd just disappeared into nothingness. Very sad, I suppose, at the thought of your little life just being abolished, the thought of Clareness going out of the world. Because while, of course, you were in most things just a little girl, reacting the way most little girls react and interested in the things most little girls are interested in, there was a kind of crumb or pellet at the centre, something that nothing would ever dissolve or wash away, that was Clare.

I'd be terribly sad if I thought that special Clareness had just been blown away into the air. I suppose that's how the rest of them feel – they don't know you're still around and they feel so sad and heavy they don't know how to bear it.

Yes, that must be it, Clare – all these grown-ups behaving in various kinds of stupid useless ways; they're acting like that because they just can't cope.

They're faced with a situation that's too much for them, and all these stupid fool things they do are just different ways of running away from it. That Smithson chap for instance – I don't believe in that anger he's always parading. He goes about pretending to be in a rage, but that's just because he can't show his real feeling, which is just plain grief. If he showed what he's really feeling he'd just sit down in a corner by himself and cry, and of course that wouldn't fit in with his machismo image, so he's pushing this anger out in front of him all the time, it's his defence, his sword and shield.

Now I see it in that light, Clare, it helps me to understand all of them a bit better. As far as I can see there isn't one of them who can cope. The Finlaysons keep it all buttoned up and laced in – the nearest they come to showing grief is to walk about looking depressed. The little fat bloke, Gerald, he's running away just as I'd guess he's run away from everything all his life, into pleasure. You go through the right motions and then you have a Good Time, because Good Times are the answer to everything.

I couldn't be like him. I don't want to be a hypocrite, though. I'm not against pleasure when it's a kind of pleasure I like. Sitting around in stuffy night-clubs drinking too much wouldn't do anything for me, nor would wolfing down ten-course meals every day and getting fat and out of breath. On the other hand a bit of sex would come in *very* handy. I've never had it away, though I've been pretty close to it a few times. I expect you know that. D'you mind my talking to you about all that? I mean, girls aren't the same, are they? It's not that they don't take an interest in sex, but it's all more, well, spread around, isn't it? I mean, I don't want to bore you and I don't want to make you feel that I'm repulsive or anything like that. It's just that, well, one has to come to terms with the fact that boys get a bit more, or let's face it, a *lot* more, steamed up over the actual mechanics of sex than girls do. I get the impression that when a boy and girl start going out, it's usually he who wants to get to the action stage. She's generally quite happy to keep it on a nice romantic warm you-and-me-together level with everybody keeping their clothes on. But he wants to get to first base. It was certainly like that with me and Libby Greenslade. I'll tell you that some time. It's pretty funny actually.

Anyway, sex, yes. Old Gerald seems to be able to get plenty of sex, at a price, but he doesn't seem to be very happy on it. That brings me back to what I was trying to say before. All these grown-ups, all running away into one kind of shelter or another. What about our two? What are they running away into?

Let me think, Clare. It's quite important to get this right. With Dad, I can never be quite sure. He just seems *soggy*. What the hell's the matter with him? Disappointment? But surely he can't be all that disappointed – I mean, he's done all right. Was he just born soggy? Somehow I don't think so. You know how just occasionally he comes to life – like, for instance, when we're all at the table and somebody says something that interests him, brings up an idea he can get hold of. His face seems to light up from inside as if something had been switched on, and all its lines change, it stops drooping and his eyes are very alive. At moments like that I've suddenly seen him as the man he might have been. What went wrong? Was it something to do with Mother? But what? On the face of it, she was a pretty good choice for him to get married to. Good looks, tall, and with more temperament than he's got. No wonder she had thoughts of going on the stage.

When I think of her by the side of that Smithson bloke, for instance, the difference I see at once is that he's pretending to feel anger but she's *really* feeling it. It goes back before what happened to you, Clare, it's been building up for years. Mother's angry, I don't know what with, but it's a cold, devouring anger that's eating away at her inside. That's the point about it, Clare, it's not eating anyone else, it's eating *her*. Is it her marriage to Dad? Frustration at never getting on the stage, boredom with Kenningbury? Just life in general? All I know is, when I see her reach for the brandy bottle, I know she isn't just trying to get pleasure from it, the way Gerald might. She's feeling aggression against the outside world and she's turning that aggression in against herself. She's saying to life, Very well, if you won't give me what I want, I'll poison myself.

And of course those times when Dad lit up, when we'd be sitting at the table among the débris of a meal and he'd start talking about something that really interested him, they were the times when the sad gulf between him and Mother was most obvious. If ever there were times when we ought to have *joined in*, all throwing something into the conversation, but letting the best-informed people talk most, and really *shared* our interests, those were the times: when we'd eaten together and were relaxed and feeling like good friends. But those were the times when Mother pulled away from Dad and went into herself and it went cold, like congealed fat on a plate.

I expect you remember, Clare, because it was only the other week – just before you went off on your trip, in fact I remember that you'd been starting to pack that afternoon, though you weren't going for two or three days, you little keenie – we had our evening meal and then we were sitting round eating apples and satsumas, and Mother was finishing up a big bottle of wine. Dad suddenly got started on the kind of big general idea he likes rambling on about. This time it was the relation of architecture to music, I'm sure you remember. I've forgotten most of what he said, in fact I hardly took much of it in, but what I do remember is how he *looked*. He pushed his wine glass away so that he could gesture without knocking it over, and he seemed to sit more lightly in his chair as if at any moment he'd spring up and start pacing about. His eyes, and his whole face, seemed *younger* suddenly.

And Mother sat opposite him, pouring herself out another glass every so often, and just let it wash over her, with no reaction. He was coming out with a lot of stuff like, 'Of course, it's obvious at the level of a common idiom between Bach and Palladio, or Purcell and Wren for that matter', and 'Pugin, on one side, leads straight to Mendelssohn, or is it the other way round?' and he kept glancing across at the gramophone and the shelf of records, as if he'd like to begin playing music and making sketches to accompany the different styles and show what he was driving at, which personally I'd have found very interesting. But then Mother, who'd got to the point in drinking where she was getting aggressive, suddenly interrupted him in this dead, bored voice, you remember? 'What tosh all this is, most architects don't know anything about music and most musicians don't know anything about architecture and couldn't care less.'

That stopped him, and the lightness seemed to go out of his body and he went back to slumping in his chair, and though he bumbled on for a bit about

a common unconscious source of inspiration, and
the Time-Spirit, and how you could see the *Bauhaus*
in Stravinsky or something of that kind, it had gone
dead on him and he soon gave up. It was as if she'd
pulled out a little rubber plug and let the air out of
him.

It left me wondering – and not for the first time,
Clare – why she did it, why she couldn't just let him
burble on, quite interestingly after all, and encourage him a bit. Developing those ideas is
quite important to him, and conversations like that
are the nearest approach to happy times as a family
that we've had for some years. It's not that she's a
bird-brain who just doesn't *like* to hear ideas
discussed, in some ways she's cleverer than the old
man and she's certainly more quick-witted. Of
course they've got different kinds of minds, he
likes to ramble on and build up structures and
speculate, he's more at ease making out the kind of
theory that you couldn't actually prove or dis-
prove, and she thinks he's too fond of hot air and
empty words. But she could sit back and enjoy it
if she wasn't so hostile to him. I suppose she's
bored by him, and feels he's messed up her life,
and she just isn't going to sit there and let him be
the star of the show. Not even the tiny little show
round the family table.

I feel better now I've talked all that out to you,
Clare, kid, listening little sister. Because of course
talking about it to someone is all I *can* do. I sure as

hell can't *do* anything for any of them, except try to understand them. That's the only kind of leadership we'll have, in the World Free Zone. It won't be who's good at commanding other people, it'll be who's good at understanding them. The person who understands most will make most decisions, and the person who makes most decisions will be leader, the only kind we have. Philosopher-kings: I came across that phrase in a book, I forget what it was, but it's stayed with me, just those two words. Philosopher-kings. That's what the World Free Zone'll need, and that's what it'll get. I'll be the first, unless someone fitter comes along, in which case fine, I'll stand down, nobody in W.F.Z.'s going to be competitive. But it's likely I'll be the first. That's why I have to learn so much, Clare. I've got to watch all these older people trying to cope with their lives and failing to and breaking down under strain and running round like rats in a tub, I've got to watch them and learn, learn, learn, learn.

Four

That familiar tap at the door. Dad again. Am I going down to dinner? Well, yes, of course I am. I'm hungry, I don't care who isn't, and if the only way to get a meal is to have it with Them, I'll do that too. We collect Mother and go down, and as we go I'm thinking: if I have dinner with them, present a united family group to the world, it'll make it easier to escape later on, I'll have paid my dues.

In the dining-room, a lot of empty places, in fact it's only about half full. I suppose a lot of them just can't face food, after all that emotion. The rest, the ones who have made it to the table, seem to be reacting the opposite way. It's as if they've suddenly realised they're starving. They reach out for dishes, hand each other this and that, get the waiter to bring more bread, pack it all away. I notice the male Finlayson getting a good solid meal down – without, of course, seeming to enjoy it, that would be too much; she isn't eating much, though.

My lot, Them, they eat just about as usual. Mother pushes her food around her plate and leaves most of it, as she generally does when she's been drinking. The old man absent-mindedly eats his way through a normal amount, neither more nor

73

less than he generally has. Somehow it all annoys me. They seem doped, not quite there, carrying on with mechanical actions through force of habit.

I look round. Mrs Richardson's sitting with Fawkes, at a little table by themselves. She looks pale but all right. She's drinking a glass of mineral water and very slowly eating olives from a glass dish. He's drinking wine. They're not speaking much but they look quiet, glad to be left alone for a bit. Which is worse, to lose a child or to settle on the person you want to live with and then to lose them? How can anybody tell? There are different kinds of love.

Here's Gerald, he's finished his telephone call, if there really was one. Little polished shoes pat, pat over the tiled floor. He's stopping by Fawkes, no, it is Mrs Richardson he's talking to, bending down with what he thinks is a kind, sympathetic smile. Actually it looks a bit greasy. He's saying something, she's saying something. Both she and Fawkes are being careful not to react too much, not to get matey with him in case he offers to join them, that's the last thing they want.

Here's the main course, thank God, big chunks of something meaty, I think it's veal. Here we go. Get this lot down and then I can escape, with a full stomach to last me till breakfast-time. Look across. Fawkes and Mrs Richardson have gone back to their non-talking quiet, Gerald's settled himself in a corner, pouring wine into a glass.

74

Would I want someone like Gerald in the World Free Zone? But then, looking round, how many of these people would be any use there? It's not fair, though, they wouldn't be such tired, useless, flaccid sad sacks if they lived in the right way. Well, but these people have a reason for being sad, for being tired. They've lost their children. That could happen in the World Free Zone, couldn't it?

I don't know. Could it?

Well, we'll have aeroplanes, won't we? And ours can have accidents like anybody else's.

Hang on a minute. We shan't need much in the way of aeroplanes. Most people will just settle down where they are. They'll be contented without rushing around the world.

But some people are bound to want to travel. There are sometimes good reasons for wanting to get about the world. And we shan't stop them because it won't be our policy to *stop* anybody doing anything.

Anything?

Well, anything normal.

So we're going to have World Free Zone airlines?

Not *as such*. It's just that the people who join in with us will all follow any occupation they want to follow. And if some of them want to run airlines, let them.

If they're successful with these airlines and they get rich, won't that put them apart from the rest of the community?

75

Why should it?

If they live in big houses with big gardens and the rest of us live in modest huts?

That's fine because, since they're the kind of people who want to live in the World Free Zone, they'll let the rest of us sit in their fine big gardens and give parties in their big houses.

Would the Finlaysons do that?

The Finlaysons wouldn't be in the World Free Zone. They're too attached to their old-fashioned ordinary orthodox way of doing things. They're too *married*.

Would married people have to get divorced if they came into the World Free Zone?

There's no need for them actually to get a piece of paper saying they were divorced. They'd just relax and forget about it, that's all. They wouldn't live in little cells with all their tensions and frustrations bouncing off the walls.

That reminds me of Them and I look from one to the other. What a waste they are, a waste of two human beings who might have come to something. Specially Mother. That pale face that would be beautiful if it wasn't so puffy and with such deep lines. And that dark red hair. I suppose there'd be quite a lot of white in it by now if she didn't use something out of a bottle. I've seen the bottle kicking about in the bathroom. Dark henna I think it's called. Pretty close to her natural colour actually. Funny neither Clare nor I inherited it.

People say I take after her; I've never been able to see it. But then I don't really look like her because I don't have any of her expressions, I don't *think* like her. I don't think like either of them. I want out. I want out.

I've finished. I'm going up to my room. One, two, three, push the chair back, stand up as naturally as possible. Dad looks up.

'You off somewhere, Paul?'

'Um.'

I want to be by myself for a bit. But it's no good bothering to explain. Just go.

Fourth report to Clare

You're still here, aren't you? Great. The reason I rushed away from dinner so fast was that I wanted to talk to you about some new ideas I've started having about the W.F.Z. Actually having them there and then, as I sat at the table among those dreary boring faces. You see, it came to me, we'll have to take the three-month probation idea a bit more seriously. Mark off the probationers from other people, not with anything that'll make them feel lowered, but just plant it quite firmly that membership of the W.F.Z. has to be *earned*.

Some distinctive clothing? No, no, this isn't a concentration camp, for God's sake.

Help me, Clare. You always were a bright little thing. I want to have some of your ideas in this, I want you to be part of the W.F.Z. even if one can't *see* you – I shall know you're there.

Let's think together.

I've got it, I don't know whether it was your idea or mine, but it's here. The difference will be a very simple one. Some dwellings, very simple dwellings of the hut type, will be set aside for the probationers and they'll be painted in a very distinctive colour – yellow, let's say. When a new person joins the World Free Zone they'll move into a yellow hut and at the end of three months they'll have decided whether they want to stay. If they do, we'll admit them formally. There could be a song written by somebody, you know, a kind of chant,

> Come out of your yellow hut,
> Come out of your yellow hut,

something about being free to choose their own colours and being free to share in everything with us. I'll work on it. But that would do, wouldn't it, Clare? I mean, old Gerald going home to his yellow hut every night, he'd start plotting and planning like hell to have a more gaily striped hut just as soon as was able to, it'd give him something to aim at. Of course we don't want competitiveness, but you can't avoid it altogether, so we'd encourage it in small things.

Of course Gerald, actual Gerald himself, I very much doubt whether we'd ever see him trying to get into the W.F.Z. The atmosphere wouldn't suit him. He'd run a mile.

Fawkes would probably fit in pretty well. What about Smithson? Hard to tell. You've noticed him, I suppose? He's pretty near to breaking up in pieces at the moment, but my guess would be that he's always pretty tense. Probably the type who wants to Get On. I'd say to look at him that he was a sales manager or something like that. You knew his daughter, I suppose, but you can't tell me about her because we haven't worked out a method yet for direct transmission of information from you to me. That'll come, I've no doubt. For the moment it's enough for me to feel that you're here. And I hope it's nice for you to *be* here. You're certainly very welcome.

You smiled then, didn't you? There wasn't anything to see, but I *felt* a smile spread through the room. It was as if, well, as if the *air* smiled.

Anyway, those are my thoughts, and meanwhile there's the problem of this evening. I tell you one thing, kid – I'm not spending it with Them. I'm going to duck out of here and be on my own, if all I do is walk about the streets. I can't stand the thought of their company, it's like a great block of concrete weighing down on my shoulders. I don't know, I'm sorry for them and all that, of course I'm sorry, I was sorry for them even before this happened but now they've got extra suffering. But I feel as if I can't reach out to them. I've outgrown them, somehow. I mean, I don't need them as parents any more, and if I did need them, that's a laugh, they just wouldn't be there. They're too absorbed in resisting one another.

I'm going out.

Five

Down the stairs. I don't bother with the little squirrel-cage lift that takes ages to come. But I'm treading warily, I want to get across the danger area of the foyer and out into the street before anybody stops me. No, correction, let's be honest, before my parents stop me.

There's a great big potted plant near the bottom of the stairs, I don't know what it's called, broad rubbery leaves. It gives me a bit of shelter and I pause for a look round. There's no one in the foyer at the moment, no, wait, Mrs Richardson's there. She's come out of the dining-room and she's standing looking at a notice of some kind on the wall. Well, she's harmless. Is Fawkes with her? He doesn't seem to be, for the moment. In any case he's harmless too, except that he might just feel he had to engage me in conversation and that'd give Them a chance to trap me.

She's still alone, the coast is as clear as it's ever going to be, let's go. But wait, here comes old Gerald out of the dining-room. He must have been watching his chance, cruising about with that triangular fin sticking up out of the water. He goes straight up to her. Neither of them is going to

notice me, I could walk straight past, but
something holds me there, at the foot of the stairs,
in the lee of the rubber-leaved plant. It's curiosity, I
suppose, I want to hear the dialogue between
them, after all, I'm here to learn about people.

'May I offer you a glass of something in the bar,
Mrs Richardson?'

She doesn't want to be hard on him, she's a nice
woman, but she clearly doesn't want to be
bothered with him. At a time like this. Or at any
time.

'Really, no, thank you.'

'Are you sure? It might help to take you out of
yourself a bit.'

That's the sort of bloody silly thing he would say.
I study her, lurking behind the leaves, as she turns
to give him the decisive heave-ho. Watch out,
Gerald, here it is.

'But, Mr . . .'

'Gerald.'

'Mr Gerald, that's just what I don't want. To be
taken out of myself.'

'I don't get it. The way I see it, you and I are the
only two who've got to face this thing alone.
Everyone else here has got a husband or wife along
with them. I was explaining earlier that my wife's a
hopeless invalid, completely bedridden. And you
. . . I just thought as we're the two lonely ones we
ought to join forces.'

She looks at him gently but very firmly. Two

nondescript people come out of the dining-room
and go past. She waits for them to get clear before
she speaks.

'I'm sorry if you're lonely, but I'm not. I feel my
husband is here with me. And if he isn't, if it's just
my imagination, that's all the more reason not to
take me out of myself.'

'*Not* to?'

'Inside myself is the only place I've got to live in
now. So I want to find out what it's like, and start
getting used to it. And I'd like to start straight
away, if it's all the same to you.'

It isn't all the same to him, he's dead disappointed, but it's too late, she's gone, and
suddenly he's turned round and seen me standing
there looking and listening.

'Well, what are you staring at?'

I wasn't ready for this. I didn't think he even
knew I was there.

'Nothing. I'm not doing anything.'

'Not much. You just saw me get the brush-off,
didn't you? Find it amusing?'

'Look, I'm not here to be amused. I'm just on my
way out.'

He looks at me with absolutely no expression. I
just can't tell what he's thinking.

'On your way out, eh? Got a bit of time on your
hands, then? Come and have a drink.'

His face has suddenly relaxed, as if in a split
second he's switched from being angry and

suspicious to being friendly, back-slapping. I don't
know which I distrust more. But he leads the way
into the bar and I follow him.

'What'll it be?'

'Lager.'

That doesn't please him. He decides to make a
thing of it.

'Lager? That's what you had last time. Why don't
you try a real drink?'

'Lager's what I generally have.'

'That's what I mean. You're abroad now. Why
don't you lash out a bit?'

He's not going to start pushing me around. I've
got my heels dug in here.

'I don't drink very often, and if I start mixing all
sorts of wines and things with the lager I've already
had, I'll be drunk and get sick. Who wants that?'

He sucks his tongue, a mockery of there-there-
little-man.

'Oh, if it's so important not to get a little drunk.'

'Yes, it is. You asked me what I'd like to drink
and I said lager. I don't have to have anything to
drink. I'll just go out and —'

'Oh, all right, all right. Don't get on your high
horse.'

He comes back from the bar with a lager for me
and an enormous whisky for himself.

'Your name's Paul, isn't it?'

'Yes.'

'Mine's Gerald.'

'I know. Well, cheers, Gerald.'

'Cheers, Paul.'

Perhaps if I just get this one down, and stay a few minutes, I'll have satisfied him and I can get out and be by myself in the velvety foreign night. I want to see Lisbon with all the lights on. I want to walk about and see what it's like at night. After all, who knows, the World Free Zone might start here. Somewhere just over the curve of the earth from here, with a cluster of huts, some yellow, some any colour you like. And at night we might walk or bicycle over and come into Lisbon and walk about in these streets with the warm pavements and walls giving off a kind of sighed-out heat. There would be music from doorways. People eating, drinking, laughing, out of doors. And perhaps . . .

But what am I thinking? Just the springtime getting into my blood and running away with me.

He's talking.

'Where d'you live, Paul?'

'Kenningbury. It's in Berkshire.'

'And what's life like in Kenningbury, Berkshire?'

'Quiet.'

This seems to amuse him. He smiles to himself a bit, drinks some more. I begin to hope I can get to the door and out. But he has another set of questions ready.

'What does your father do, Paul?'

'He's an architect.'

'Does he like being in Kenningbury, Berkshire? I

mean does he like a quiet life?'

'I expect so. We don't discuss it.'

'And what about you, Paul? Do you like a quiet life?'

There doesn't seem to be anything worth saying in answer to this, so I just give a shrug. He leans forward with the whisky glass held tight in his podgy hand.

'But there are times when you wonder what's going on out there, eh? When you feel like breaking out?'

I shrug again. Even if I did feel like this, what's it to him? But he really seems to want to know.

'You're young, Paul. Don't you want to start finding out about life?'

'All right, I'm young.'

'Well?'

'Well what? I'm here because my sister got killed in the crash. I'm here to take part in the church service and try to be a help to my parents. That's finding out above life, isn't it?'

He's nodding, I've scored a point of some kind anyway.

'I see all that, Paul, of course. But I wonder if you've considered the question of how to *deal* with a sorrow like this. I mean, when you've done all the right things, gone to the right places, said the right words, what then?'

'What then? Go home and get on with your life, I suppose.'

'No.'

He's shaking his head. He really means it, whatever 'it' will turn out to be.

'There's a stage before that. A stage that comes between the observance of grief and the ordinary life taking over. You've forgotten the wake.'

'The wake?'

'Yes, the good old custom that after you'd buried somebody, given them a slap-up funeral with all the right prayers and psalms and the right feelings, you cut up. Everybody joined in and had a good time.'

I look round at the empty bar, and there seems to be nothing to say except:

'Well, that isn't going to happen this time, is it? Everybody *isn't* joining in.'

He flaps his hand in a gesture that means, to hell with them.

'All right, they're not joining in. They've got it all wrong. That holier-than-thou, touch-me-not Richardson woman. I could tell her a thing or two. Hah. Yes, I could. But look. It doesn't matter to me what the rest of them do, I know I'm right. I'm looking for a wake.'

'Oh?'

'I know this town. I know the spots where you can really enjoy yourself.'

'Oh?'

'The paper I work for is very good about expenses. When any of our chaps go abroad, they

87

don't have to be too finicky about what expenses
they put down. The paper knows it benefits in the
end. If the chaps get out and about a bit, see some
life, get to meet the people who make things
hum. . . . Well, that's where the stories are.'

I don't know what to say and I must say
something, so I say: 'I didn't know you worked for
a paper.'

'I work for the *Flash*. Was a reporter for years.
Covered every kind of news story. I'm getting slow
now, so I leave that to the younger men. I'm in
management now, mostly. But once a newspaperman, always a newspaperman.'

He's chuckling to himself, as if there's some joke
knocking about, a joke that he can see and I can't.
So what, I don't want his lousy jokes. I want to get
rid of him and go out. But God, it's proving
difficult. He seems to have some big plan in mind.
Now he's leaning towards me again.

'It seems to me, young Paul, that I could take you
out this evening and show you a few sides of life
that probably aren't there in Kenningbury,
Berkshire.'

I want to tell him to get lost, but something's
holding me back. After all, even he . . . I mean
even he might be a means of . . . I'm here to learn,
perhaps I shouldn't turn away from any chance to
go anywhere, find out about anything.

'I can't go out on the town. I've no money.'

He waves that pudgy hand again.

'My paper allows me generous expenses.'

'But you're not working for them. You're on this trip for your own purposes, not theirs.'

He ducks that one.

'A newsman is never off duty. Who knows when there might be a story. Look, there was an earthquake in Lisbon in 1750, one of the biggest ever in Europe. Suppose there was one tonight? And I survived it and telephoned a description? It's always worth a paper's while to have an experienced man *anywhere*.'

I'm not arguing.

'Now listen here, Paul. I'm going to take you out and show you Lisbon. The *other* Lisbon. The side that isn't like Kenningbury, Berkshire.'

To gain a little time, I say: 'Anywhere in particular?'

'To a nightclub called Tina's. They know me there. We'll get a good welcome.'

I'm still playing for time, but by now I know it's settled, I'm going with him.

'And what goes on at Tina's nightclub?'

'Everything.'

It's settled. He's standing up.

'I have to go to my room to get credit cards and things. You'd better go and find your parents, hadn't you?'

Find my parents. That's a laugh. As if they'd have enough enterprise to get lost!

'That won't be necessary.'

'Well, but you'll need to tell them you're going out and might be late getting in.'

'That won't be necessary.'

'Won't they worry?'

'No.'

Now it's his turn to shrug. He goes to the lift. I wait.

Fifth report to Clare

Yes, I know you're here. I could feel you standing close to me all the time I was going through all that chat with him. And now, without even waiting for me to be in a room by myself or out in the street, you're beside me as I stand here in the foyer, looking out through the plate-glass doors at the night settling down on the city and the people walking by and, beyond them, the ten lanes of traffic.

You're worried, that's why you're sort of plucking at my sleeve, and yes, I can see it all, I understand. It horrifies my sister to see me agreeing to go off into the night with a fat sweaty hog like him. You think it's the first step to me turning into a hog myself. Well, relax, Clare, forget all worries of that kind. Whatever happens in the next few hours is just going to be information-gathering. You see, one thing old Gerald said is perfectly true and nobody could deny it: there are a hell of a lot of things, some of them pretty normal human activities, that don't go on in Kenningbury, Berkshire.

Yes, I know what you're thinking – that this place he's taking me to will turn out to be a whore-house.

Well, I can tell you definitely. One, I am not going for that reason. Two, if it does turn out that way, and even if I do finish up having over-the-counter sex, it isn't going to make any difference to me deep down. It isn't going to alter anything. I mean, one has to deal with this sex business one way or another. I sometimes get pretty randy and, of course, there's nothing doing at Kenningbury. (If you can see the past as clearly as you can see the present, you'll know what happened with Libby Greenslade – or rather what *didn't* happen. But you won't want me to waste time looking back on that, especially now.) I suppose if I lived in London or somewhere with a more swinging scene, I'd have had plenty of chances by now and being a normal person I'd have taken some of them. I think about it enough, perhaps it's time I found out what it's like at first hand. But in a way, Clare, that's a detail. It might be better for the first time to be with someone who's very used to it, takes it as a matter of course, rather than with some girl of my own age who's just as inexperienced as me and much more nervous. But whether it happens or not doesn't *matter*.

Because all that matters, Clare, is that I should *learn*. I've got a very big job to do, one of the biggest there is. I'm going to establish the World Free Zone, and be in sole charge of it for the first few years at least, for the simple reason that there'll be no one else to do it. When enough other people get the hang of it, somebody more fitted to be Number One might emerge, and believe me I'll be glad to step down. But till then I've got to be on top of every situation, I've got to foresee everything and know all the angles, and that means that I've got to know just about everything, even the kind of things Gerald knows.

You do see that, Clare, don't you? And you will come with me?

That's good. I'm ready now.

Six

Where the hell's Gerald? I thought he'd be about two minutes, but he's been five or six already and I'm standing here, looking out into the street, right in the way of everybody's comings and goings.

That's settled it with Clare, anyway, I'm sure she understands now how I see the situation and why I'm going out with Gerald rather than just hanging about by myself. But I was hoping to duck out without having to explain anything to Them, and now it's too late, I'm trapped, they've seen me.

Out of the dining-room they come, trailing along, my parents and the Finlaysons and a couple of strays I don't know the names of. They must have been sitting over the remains of dinner, trying to cheer one another up a bit, and now they're facing the evening and not sure how they'll be able to get through it. The Finlaysons, of course, are very composed, they were born composed and they'll die composed, and Mother's putting on a good face as she always does in public, she gives me a smile but walks past without trying to buttonhole me, she knows if I've anything to say to her I'll come and say it.

But the old man, that's different, he's bringing

up the rear and looks hang-dog, pathetic.

Of course I'm sorry for him, in a way, though it's all his own fault for letting everything slide into such a mess, and of course I know what it is he's afraid of. He thinks – correction, he *knows* – Mother will hit the bottle and disappear into dreamland, and he'll be left staring at the wallpaper. He wants company, and mine'll do.

But the answer is No. I'm *not* going to spend the evening with him and I'm *not* going to tell him where I'm going or who with or what I'm doing or anything about it. My life is my own and I'm going to live it, beginning now.

Here it comes. Brace myself to tread on him.

'Oh, there you are, Paul.'

'Yes, here I am.'

Hesitation, then:

'Thinking of going out?'

Don't say anything. No lies, no raising false hopes, nothing.

'I thought we might ... have a bit of a stroll round together. You know, take a look at the city and ... sit and have a glass of something and watch the world go by.'

'I don't think I will, thanks.'

You've said it now, there's nothing needs to be added. Duck into some sort of shelter till he goes away. Where? Ah, there's a toilet or something just back there. Picture of a little man and a little woman.

'Excuse me.'

Dart off. Leave him standing there.

It's cool in here, a tap dripping, hand-drier, neutral space, sanctuary. Give it a couple of minutes.

He'll have cleared off now.

I feel sorry for him, of course I do. One of the foundations of the World Free Zone is compassion, for *anybody* who's miserable for any reason.

But not only compassion. To be with us, people must be something more than just miserable. They must be contributing. He's not contributing.

Open the door, out, look around, the coast's clear. Oh, there's Gerald. He's waiting, with a neat little overcoat across his arm, looking round impatiently.

'Where've you been?'

'Just having a pee.'

'All right, let's get on the move.'

He tells the porter we shall need a taxi. The porter's old, bald, decrepit, but he can do that much. He goes out into the street and in a moment a taxi's standing there by the kerb, in another moment we're in it, Gerald's giving an address and we're off.

Off where?

Gerald seems to know, he's sitting back with his cocky little curly-brim hat tilted a little to one side, fag in his mouth, oh, he's the cool one. The man about town, all ready to take pity on the poor inexperienced adolescent from Kenningbury, Berkshire, who hasn't seen anything yet.

Poor silly sod, he hasn't a clue about what's really going on. This is the founder of the World Free Zone he's dealing with. Not some trembling adolescent who can't wait to be shocked and jolted and thrown into the deep end of the mud-bath of life, but rather just information-gathering, coolly and methodically filling in gaps. Yes, I'm seventeen, yes, I come from a quiet middle-class background in a quiet middle-class area, I'm quite aware of the fact that I'm going into the sort of place and among the sort of people I've never seen before, but what Gerald doesn't realise is that there's no need to be sweaty about it. Pretty well every day I live, *something* happens to me for the first time.

He can't realise that because to him it's all so important, pleasure, having a good time, kicking over the traces, though it's a long time since there were any traces for him to kick over.

He's talking, he's bragging about his paper.

'The old *Flash* has had its critics, of course. Its enemies, even. But one thing nobody's ever accused it of is being mean. They know when to spend money wisely.'

'Yes?'

'I've gone all over the world for them. Twenty years as a reporter. Now I'm more on the management side, but I still do a fair bit of travelling. And wherever I've been, I've always just sent in my expenses to them and they've paid up without a murmur.'

'Sounds good.'

'It *is* good, laddie. If your chaps have a bit of money in their pockets which they're not afraid to spend, they get out and about. Involved in Life a bit.'

The sort of life your paper wants to know about, anyway. I keep that thought to myself and just grunt.

'That's how you get on to stories. There's no other way, in fact. And what stories! I could tell you a thing or two.'

I hope he won't.

This taxi ride's going on and on. I was hoping wherever we were going to wouldn't be far away, so if I get too damn bored I can just cut out and walk back to the hotel. I knew it wouldn't be easy to shake Gerald off, but it would have been nice to keep in mind as a possibility. But this doesn't look very possible. We've gone up hills and down hills, and through lighted squares with crowds in them, and now we're going down a long cavern-like street with not many people about at all, and it seems to go on and on for miles.

These streets in southern towns. Narrow as hell. Tiny little pavements with only just room for one person on them, so that you're always having to step into the gutter or shove someone else into it.

Must be to beat the heat. There must be months when life's only tolerable if you can keep in the shade. Takes a bit of imagining in Kenningbury, Berkshire.

Gerald's talking to the taxi-driver. Does that mean he's given up on me already? Or is he just trying to show off that he knows a bit of Portuguese? But no, of course, I remember now, he has to keep talking to everybody he meets, or one day he might miss a Story. Perhaps the bloke's on his way to assassinate a cabinet minister and if Gerald doesn't talk to him he'll never hear about it. What a load of crap.

'Something, something, *aberto*.'

He's asking a question. About the place we're going to? The driver's reassuring him.

'Sim.'

Even I know what that means. Then something, something, *aberto* again. I get it. *Aberto* must mean open. Gerald's wondering if this nightspot'll have its doors open as early as this and what the hell we're going to find to talk about, him and me, if it hasn't. The driver seems to think it's always *aberto*.

Well, we're going to find out now, because we're stopping, we've stopped, we've got out, Gerald's paying, and this pale blue neon sign, a bit erratic, a bit winking, says 'Tina's'.

Here we go up the stairs. Get ready to have your life changed, Master Paul. Get ready for everything to seem different, bathed in a new light, from this

99

evening on. Like hell. Just an ordinary crummy, sleazy nightspot, the kind Gerald's spent his life looking round for and finding, telling himself he was getting Life. Well, all information is worth having. The W.F.Z. can best be launched by someone who's seen *everything*.

Seen? Only seen? What about done?

We can see about that as we go along. At the moment I'm in an observing mood.

We're in, Gerald's checking his hat and coat in, I do the same, and now we're walking into the one long room the place seems to consist of. On the surface, anyway. Dim lighting, lots of red bulbs, a long bar going right down one side with stools, the rest of it benches and little tables, some of the floor space kept clear: for dancing? There's a juke-box. Can't see much detail in the cruddy light. Good God, is he going to spend the whole evening in this hole? Is that his idea of living it up? It's more fun at the Kenningbury Youth Club.

What's Gerald up to? He's having an argument with the barman. Young bloke in a white coat. He's ordered drinks and the barman is telling him to sit down. They flounder a bit, with Gerald trying to get through in Portuguese for the sake of appearances, then go into English. The barman knows it better than Gerald knows Portuguese, at any rate. They start arguing the toss all over again.

'As I said, a large whisky and a glass of lager.'

'No bar service, *senhor*.'

'What d'you mean, no bar service. You're standing there and I'm standing here. A Scotch and a lager, please.'

'Look, mister, no bar service. You sit down, the young lady bring you everything you want.'

The place is dead empty. No young lady, no old lady, no anybody except this jowly young barman in his white coat. Gerald decides to be the kindly uncle.

'Look, laddie, I'm well known here. Just step into the back room and tell Tina I'm here.'

'Sit *down*, mister, and the young lady — '

'Tell her Gerald's here. Gerald, from London. Look, don't just *stand* there. Go and tell Tina — '

'Who Tina? Who you mean, Tina?'

'Tina, for God's sake. The madam ... the manageress.'

I'm beginning not to like this, standing in this long, empty room where we could have our throats cut and nobody any the wiser, and Gerald trying to come it over this bloke who looks as if he might be the chucker-out as well as the barman. He puts his hands flat on the bar as if he's getting ready to vault over it, and raises his voice a good deal.

'No Tina! Nobody here name Tina!'

'But surely she's — '

'YOU SIT DOWN!'

We sit down. Gerald goes through the motions of choosing the best spot, settling in comfortably, but it's pretty obvious we're sitting down because if we don't the barman'll knock us down. But the shouting-match seems to have alerted other people in the building, got it through to them that some customers have started arriving. A door opens at the end of the room and two girls come in. They're wearing net stockings and little frilly skirts. Elaborate hair-dos. They walk over slowly and sit down on bar stools, talk to the barman for a bit, and then one of them comes and stands in front of us. Doesn't speak any English, it seems. But Gerald's confidence surges back, now that somebody's taking notice of him.

He goes through the routine of ordering drinks and even scrapes up a bit of Portuguese to chat the girl along. She just stands there, taking the order down on a little pad, taking no notice of his patter. Her make-up's careless. You can see the streaks where she's put the powder on in great swaths, not bothering. Everything about her says *Screw you, Jack*. I rather like her for it.

This is wonderful. It's all going so well. The man who's brought me here is horrible, but *there was no other way to find out*. Find out what? My own strength, of course, what my values really add up to. The World Free Zone is going to be rock-solid. I know that now, and how do I know it? Because at last it's happened, I've been put down in front of these Temptations they all babble on about, the things that make people go back on their beliefs and let down their friends, and I've taken their measure and they're nothing, well, not nothing, but not enough. My life has a purpose, I'm giving it to the World Free Zone, and I know now that nothing's going to hold me up on the way, no snare will be able to catch me – I know it because these are the snares, they're here, I'm looking at them and they're not enough.

He's yakking away, leaning towards me, I can see his mouth moving under his silly little moustache and I can't be bothered to take in what he's saying. Something about Charlie. I can quite see it's rough on him, loving the boy, but I can't feel sorry for him because his only idea was to produce a carbon copy of himself, just as doggy and know-it-all and up to the same dirty tricks. A disaster if he'd succeeded. And if he hadn't, if the boy had reacted against him, tried to turn himself into a completely different person, what a struggle he'd have had with this old sod on his back.

Yes, sit there, you silly vulgar fat little man, one of evolution's failures, with your sweaty forehead and your podgy little legs only just reaching the floor. Sit there talking away, laying it down, so sure of yourself, cocky. There's so much you don't know. To start with, you don't know a thing about what's going on in my mind. You think you're being a benefactor to me, helping me to get to know the score, initiating me into a side of life I'm not likely to find in Kenningbury, Berkshire. You're great on sides of life, aren't you, Gerald? That's because you keep everything in separate trays. As a boy grows up he's ready for this tray and then that tray. Doesn't seem to occur to you that people don't grow up in that prefabricated way.

God, the scunge of this place. I bet if the lighting was good enough to take a proper look at the glasses they'd be all over greasy fingermarks. The whole place is one big greasy fingermark, come to that. The canned music, coming over a bit blurred and a bit too loud, isn't giving atmosphere, it's taking it away. The girls lounging against the bar are a used-up looking lot, even the youngest of them. There are five or six of them now, and not one I'd like to get with, however randy I was feeling.

Oh, I feel sorry for you, Gerald. Is this that big glamorous life of pleasure you think is so important? Is this what your paper spends so much money on, shelling out on expenses so that the chaps who work for it can see another side of life?

He's still talking. Some of it begins to get through. Not that he seems to care much whether I'm listening or not, as long as I don't interrupt and just let him get it off his chest.

'I never saw enough of Charlie. Not my fault. It was the wife. Kept me away from him as if I'd got typhoid or something.'

'Oh.'

'Had a lot of trouble with her. All that guff I hand out about my wife being a hopeless invalid,

bedridden and all that, it's just for this lot here. Just
for the school. I wanted to keep that as my
preserve, make sure they never invited her to
anything. You see, it was my only link with
Charlie.'

'Yes?'

'Yes. The wife and I had split up. I was what you
might call, in the habit of enjoying myself.
Especially when I took trips abroad, which was
quite frequently. I thought she didn't know about
it, or that it didn't bother her, but one Monday
morning when I got back I found she'd set the
lawyers on me. She'd got everything ready – had it
all planned for months.'

'Oh.'

'Yes. Have another lager, if you won't have
anything else. Waitress! Here, my dear – um
Scotch, *grande e una cerveza*, lager. Yes, she'd even
got a new husband waiting in the wings. Nice quiet
boring type who does the garden and smokes a
pipe and sits in front of the box every evening while
she darns his socks. It's all he wants, so let him get
on with it. But I was out – out on my ear. She
chased me away with a garden fork if I ever went
near the house. And that meant I never saw the
kids. The two girls I don't mind about so much,
they'll grow up in their own way, but Charlie, I
couldn't stand that.'

'No?'

'I felt he needed me to help him grow up and I

105

wasn't going to leave it to that walking herbaceous border she'd settled down with.'

'Um.'

'So I got him to Ironstone. Cost a bomb but I never begrudged it. I could always get down to see him at weekends. I used to take him out for a drive on Sunday afternoons. Wind up eating cream buns somewhere. He'd have been into something better than cream buns in another year or two.'

'Hah.'

You're so wrong, Gerald, so wrong. It would all just have been cream buns, cream buns till the end of time. At least I've got that to thank you for. You've shown me the cream buns lying there on the plate and I know I can get along without them.

Here's my lager and Gerald's whisky. I don't really want mine, I've got half the last lot left, and I'm *not going to be hurried*. I'm going to bed sober tonight.

From the official memoir of the Founder:
The Founder was not what is ordinarily known as an ascetic. His warm sympathy extended to all types of human need, including the needs of the flesh. Indeed, his successful relationships with women, detailed in the standard biography by Dr Titmuss, indicate that he had a deep intuitive grasp of the feminine nature and understood sexual love in all its fullness. What he had no time for, what repelled him, was promiscuity.

Gerald's dashing back his whisky. Seems

desperate to get enough alcohol into his system. Is it to deaden pain? Ought I to feel sorry for him? I suppose so, and yet ... this place, the tawdriness, the awful mound of grot it all is, stands between me and feeling anything.

The Founder's recoil from vice, his dislike of mere sensual gratification, began early in life. He would sometimes refer to a formative youthful experience in Lisbon, when a well-meaning but stupid older companion offered to initiate him into the life of pleasure; 'I was like a child let loose in a sweetshop,' he would recall with his characteristic benign smile, 'and I didn't want to dive my hand into any of the boxes or jars. It was, quite simply, the wrong kind of temptation for a person constituted as I am.'

Gerald's saying something. Lean forward, hear him over the canned music. Might as well observe the courtesies.

'How old are you, Paul?'

Oh, Christ. Here we go. He's going to get all personal, and warm and sweaty, and I'm going to be the substitute for his lost son.

'I'm seventeen.'

'Seventeen. Charlie was just coming up to fifteen.'

'Um.'

'Another two years, just think of it, he'd have been like you. Damn near grown-up.'

'Um.'

'In fact in most ways I s'pose you *are* grown up. God, I can remember myself at seventeen. That was when I left school and became a cub reporter. Worked for a news agency first. I must have worked hard. You didn't get started in any other way then. Early fifties I'm talking about, God, it seems a long time ago. Before any of the modern things got going. Most people didn't have TV. Bill Haley hadn't started rock-and-roll, never mind the Beatles. You couldn't imagine it. No union making up reasons why you couldn't do a hand's turn without double time and weighting. We were in the N.U.J. of course, but it was kid's stuff compared with now. All night I worked. But when I look back, I don't remember the work. It's gone. All those hours of hard slog, pulling yourself up the ladder rung by rung, it's all forgotten. Vanished. When I look back at myself when I was seventeen, all I remember is . . .'

Wait for it. He's going to say something important. Important to him, that is. He drops his voice to a growl and leans forward.

'Crumpet.'

He's come out with it. He's sitting back as if a difficult task has been accomplished. Difficult, but necessary. He's done it, he's brought out that one sacred word! Crumpet!

'All I cared about when I was seventeen.'

He's off again. Pretend to be listening. Sip some lager. Filthy, sudsy stuff. *The Founder would often recall an experience in Lisbon.*

'I'll be frank. I'll be honest with you, Paul, just as I'd be honest with . . .'

I think he was going to say, Charlie. But he stopped. Now he's starting again.

'I'll be honest with you. When I was seventeen I never got it out of sight. Never got within a million miles of it. But *in my mind*, that was just about all that was happening. Everything else was a dream. The only real thing in my life was crumpet. Not the crumpet I was having, because that didn't exist. But the crumpet I was *going* to get when I got a bit older, and started earning more, and getting my chances.'

He's leaning forward again. This is very important to him. Why the hell is it so important?

'Now, Paul, don't tell me you're any different. Don't tell me you think seriously about anything else.'

Oh, shove off.

'Of course, times have changed. Young people have more freedom now. For all I know, you're getting it away already.'

This has got to stop. I put my lager glass down and look straight at him.

'Why does it matter what I'm getting?'

He thinks this one over, gets a bit truculent.

'Who said it matters?'

'All right. Perhaps you wouldn't mind if I just . . . kept myself out of it.'

'All right. Keep yourself out of it if you like. But remember this, Paul. Just remember this as a principle in life. If you don't move towards people, they won't move towards you.'

'All right.'

'If you keep yourself clammed up, very tight, and you don't make any move towards people who've offered you their confidence . . . you'll find that they'll clam up too.'

I've hurt him, I can see that. But what on earth could I have done? Start swopping a lot of greasy confidences? I couldn't bear that, and anyway I haven't any to swop. Poor old Libby Greenslade's hardly Gerald material.

Say something mollifying, though. He's in enough pain as it is.

'Look, I'd tell you about myself if there was anything to tell. But there isn't. My life hasn't started yet.'

'Not started?'

'No. I just come home from school every day and do my homework and then have supper and probably watch a bit of television or read something and then I go to bed. The next day it all starts up again. I don't actually do anything.'

He's nodding.

'I see. You're like me at your age. You're working, working, working, but behind that your mind's on the things that really matter.'

'I don't know where my mind is. It's here, it's

there, it's everywhere.'

What I mean is that I'm not telling *him* where my mind is. Good God! Fancy trying to tell him about the World Free Zone!

One of the girls from the bar comes over and stands behind Gerald, with her hand on the back of his chair. He takes no notice. He's looking at me, really looking attentively as if he's seeing me for the first time.

'You know, Paul, I think I had you wrong.'

'Had me wrong?'

'Yes. I thought it was all going to be much easier.'

'*What* was going to be easier?'

'Getting to know you. Taking you out of yourself.'

The girl goes away again. Gerald's still staring at me.

'You're more deeply inside yourself than ever, aren't you? You're in that thick shell and you haven't come out an inch. Can you tell me what's the matter?'

The problem is, how to be frank with him. I mean, there's no need to take him on a conducted tour of what's actually going on in my mind. It wouldn't be possible anyway. Still, I've got to say something and that something ought to be true even if it doesn't gather up the whole truth.

'I'm not quite sure whether I'm in my shell. Perhaps I just give that impression, perhaps that's just the kind of person I am. But I can say one thing, this place isn't helping.'

He looks round at the long room with its strip lighting and its deep shadows and the long sad bar. At that moment a gang of men come in, noisily, laughing and shouting to one another. Gerald's taking them in along with the rest.

'Greek sailors. That's my guess. I think this place has gone down since Tina left. Yes, that must be it. Tina must have gone and the place is just rolling downhill!'

He gets up, suddenly.

'Come on.'

'Come on? Where?'

The Greek sailors are really whooping it up. The girls are looking more cheerful.

'I'm curious to find out if there's any place in this town that you *would* like. Any place of the nightspot kind, that is. And I think I know the very one. Somewhere very different from here. Come on, I'll get the coats.'

So now he's got them and we're going down the stairs and out. We walk through the streets for ten minutes or so, this isn't a taxi job, all these places must be pretty much in the same part of town. As we pass different clubs and what-not, very often with touts hanging about outside, trying to talk you into going in, Gerald describes them, or at any rate puts them into categories; this is a Japanese one, that's mainly Americans; the Roma, all the girls there are Italian. What a lot he knows, what a hell of a lot of rubbish.

So now we're going into a discreetly lit hallway, this is a much more plushy place, and there's no need for Gerald to draw on his odds and ends of Portuguese, as soon as he speaks to them in English they answer in English. I can see this place is going to cost him a mint. I hope it's worth it, just to impress me. But I have a hunch it is worth it.

You sit at tables here, and there's a kind of stage area for the floor-show. It isn't raised, it's just a roped-off area of polished floor, and in the middle of it are some panes of glass, like a window only lying flat, with soft light coming up through them. A bloke like a head waiter takes charge of us. V.I.P. treatment. Red carpet. Makes me feel like a walking credit card.

We're at our table, we've got drinks – I'm sticking to lager, no matter *what* he says – and I can settle back and look round. This place is certainly different from the last one, I'll give it that. Not at bottom, I suppose – everybody here's after the same things, as Gerald would no doubt say – but very definitely on the surface. It's a posh, expense-account joint. Some of the chaps here are actually in evening dress, for God's sake. At least that's what I suppose it is when they're dressed like penguins. A clean shirt to go with a dirty mind. And of course I can read Gerald's. His mind, not his shirt. I can see all the way down to the floor of his mind – it's like looking into a cattle-trough after they've finished drinking from it, frothing and dropping snot and stuff in the water. He could see the other place wasn't impressing me, so he thought he'd open his wallet a bit further, spend some real money and see if that did the trick. It's become a matter of pride with him to make me think how marvellous the big wicked world of pleasure is, and how smashing it would be if I could only afford to join it, to come to places like this every night. Poor sod. He doesn't realise I'm a completely different kind of human being. It's not that I'm puritanical, I'm not an aseptic or whatever they call it, *ascetic*, that's it. *The Founder was not averse to ordinary human pleasures; in particular he took joy in the company of women, as his many warm and lasting relationships bear witness*, blah, blah. I'm sure that's how it'll be. I shall enjoy sex very much, when it happens to me to get some. Libby Greenslade. Oh, God. Makes me go hot and cold. Why didn't we manage it? Was it my fault? I don't really think so and in any case I'm not going to blame myself. It was just straight inexperience on both sides, that's all. Next time, whenever there is a next time, it'll probably be a breeze. Specially if I can get together with somebody a bit more worldly-wise than poor old Libby. I wonder if she'll ever make it with anybody. She should do, she's quite good-looking. It's just that she's so vague. Looking back, I wonder sometimes if she even knew what the hell we were trying to *do*.

Gerald's still fed up because I'm not making conversation. Well, it is pretty unfriendly of me, I suppose. He's spending money trying to give me a good time, I ought to come on a bit more. The trouble is, I know deep down it isn't me he's trying to give a good time to, it's his son, Charlie, his lost son. The point is, if he takes me to the sort of place he was planning to take Charlie to and I'm not impressed, he feels he's let Charlie down somehow. So he's brought me to this place which means when he gets home he'll have to pawn the family jewels, to damn well *make* me sit up.

And I'm just as bored as ever because he's missing the point about me and all the people like me there are in the world.

Well, let's make conversation. The evening can't last for ever, even if it lasts till tomorrow morning. Tomorrow morning. Tomorrow by tea-time I'll be back in Kenningbury, Berkshire. What a strange thought. How extraordinary this place is going to seem when I think back to it from Kenningbury, and how absolutely Martian Kenningbury seems when I think about it from here – but they're both on the same earth, and so is the World Free Zone, though at the moment it's just an idea inside my head. I wriggle forward a bit on my chair, so Gerald can hear me over the piped music and the buzz of talk, and get my mouth into some sort of motion.

'Bit of a change, this place.'

'A change?'

'Very different from the other one.'

He waves his fat little hand as if to dismiss the other place.

'Oh, yes, Tina's. Not in the same class as this. Of course you've got to be fair. It was offering a different set of goods.'

He's always got to be *explaining* things to me. Now my boy for your next lesson you will swot up this, that, the other. So I just play it along.

'Yes?'

'Yes.'

He's sitting back, looking wise. Little fat Philosopher-king.

'Not to put too fine a point on it, Tina's is a knock-shop.'

'And this isn't?'

He shakes his head.

'Not in the same way. There are girls for sale here, if you know which ones to ask and what procedures to go through, but they're freelances and they're very expensive. At Tina's you could have any of the girls who were sitting along the bar for the equivalent of about, say twenty quid. That's their job and no one pretends anything else. The screwing in a place like this is more a matter of free-market enterprise, you might say.'

This is the sort of thing I'm supposed to learn if I want to Enjoy Myself. Thank God I don't want to. But let him talk.

'I could see the girls down at Tina's didn't make

much appeal to you.'

If he means I didn't want to fuck them, he's right. But I suddenly think how horrible it is for him to be sitting here, talking about those girls in that patronising way, treating them like market cattle. They're *people*, and I can tell you something, Gerald, there might very well be girls like that in the W.F.Z. but there won't be anyone remotely like *you*.

He's settling back, cradling his whisky. Now he's looking at his watch.

'Nearly eleven. The cabaret should be starting any time.'

'Cabaret?'

'They make a bit of a speciality of it here.'

Oh, well, might as well just go along with the whole thing. I've never watched a cabaret but I suppose it's just a series of turns, the sort of thing you'd see on television, only with the girls wearing a bit less.

Sure enough, it starts. And sure enough I was right about the girls wearing less. They come on to this tiny area with the lighted window-panes under it and some bloke at the far end of the room starts drenching it in coloured lights of various kinds. Strobe, I think it's called. Every so often he gets to ordinary clear light and holds it for a few moments, so you get a good look, and then goes back into red, orange, blue, yellow.

We've got a good view, V.I.P. seats at our little

117

table, leave it to good old Gerald, hang around him
and you'll be all right. All right as long as you don't
mind getting it all wrong. And for this evening I
don't mind at all. It's a useful test. *Our Founder was
not puritanical. He was against the mere exploitation of
women, but he was not against happiness, love,
sensuality even. Here is a rare photograph of our
Founder, in youth, taken in a Lisbon cabaret. He
described it later as an exploratory visit.* Yes,
exploratory. There seem to be three run-of-the-mill
chorus girls and two others who are the stars. In
this first scene, the two stars are keeping their
clothes on, for the time being anyway, but the three
troupers seem to have shed most of theirs before
coming on. When the light goes natural, everybody
gets a good eyeful. Hang around good old Gerald if
you're interested in nipples. I'm very reassured
because I find it exciting (so I'm normal) but not so
much as to drive me wild (so I'm in control).

That turn's over, we get some more drinks – shall
I ever get the soapy feel of lager out of my mouth? –
and then a Spanish-looking bloke comes on and
does some conjuring tricks, while the man on
the strobe lighting takes a break. They're good
tricks, very baffling, quick, precise, skilful. This
is the kind of entertainer we'll want a lot of in the
W.F.Z.

Yes, the evening's going by quite pleasantly.
Having something to watch is a good way of not
having to talk to old Gerald. (Sudden thought: was

that idea in *his* head too? Does he find *me* boring?
Well, he would, of course. I wonder what Charlie
was really like, whether he was a miniature Gerald,
or was trying to grow up into somebody quite
different, poor little sod.)

It's all fine, I'm sitting back, and this place at any
rate doesn't smell dusty, as that other one did:
dusty and a bit sweaty. My lager glass is three-
quarters full and it's going to be the *last one*. I'm in
control, Paul Waterford's in the driving seat.

The chap with the coloured lights is at it again
and this time he's got an effect of bubbles moving
upwards, as if the scene's going to be set in a bottle
of soda water. Oh, no, I get it now, it's under the
sea. The great big world of the ocean. God, they're
really trying with this one. The canned music's all
mysterious and echo-ey, like something you'd hear
in an underwater cavern. Well, they're trying. Now
here come the three girls dressed as sea-horses,
with those curled-up tails and big head-dresses,
well at least it's obvious what they're supposed to
be. You couldn't actually *mistake* them for sea-
horses because sea-horses don't have tits, and if
they did have them they probably wouldn't bother,
in all that cold water, to flash them around the way
these three are doing. Well, they're working hard
for their money, and if only everyone did that the
world'd go round a lot more smoothly.

Ah, what's this? Some drama. A story-line. Into
this charming sea-horse scene comes a girl in

underwater hunting get-up. I recognise her, she's one of the two stars of the show, but in the first scene she really didn't do anything but walk on and I didn't take much notice of her. Now she's the centre of attention.

The centre of attention.

Attention. Tension. Attention. Tension. Centre. Scent her. Tension.

God, what's happening to me?

She's a blonde, a lot of hair, sort of bushed out all round her head; big eyes; a rather long face, long upper lip, sensitive-looking mouth with a pronounced Cupid's bow. Long, slender arms and legs, long slender body. And her get-up. Flippers on her feet to keep up that underwater illusion. Strapped to her thigh, one of those underwater spear-guns, can't see from here whether it's a real one or a plastic mock-up. Underwater goggles, but she's got them pushed up on to the top of her head so that you can see her face, and to hell with realism.

She's moving about in that gas-bubble light. I'm going to try to take my eyes off her. I'm going to try to take my eyes off her. My eyes off her. My eyes off her.

I can't.

Realism, realism, she's wearing a costume that must be exactly the kind, it must have come from a marine sports outfitter, it's heavy black rubber edged with red, but where the realism breaks down

120

is that surely if she was underwater she'd keep it zipped up, it's got a heavy zip right down the front and she's working it open bit by bit, now you can see her breasts or almost see them, almost see them, about half the nipple on one side, about half the nipple on the other, she has these very developed, very prominent nipples, rather dark in colour, is it the lighting, I must watch, I must wait through all the changes of light, I must see them, I must see them

I don't think I'm going to be able to stand this

The three sea-horse girls go off and she's left onstage alone and the lights move to normal just ordinary bright clear light and she wiggles her zip right down to her navel and her breasts are the only two things there are in the world the only two things there are in the

Now they're coming back and they're carrying something and the lighting is underwater again, complete with bubbles, but I still can't take my eyes off her and the zip's down to her waist. What is it they're carrying, oh, it's a rubber shark, a blown-up fun thin thing with a *Jaws* face. They bring it towards her, the canned music changes and gets dramatic, Fight to the Death sort of thing, they swing it about above her head and now she's pulled the spear out of the gun on her thigh, it must be a toy one so as not to burst the shark, and she's wrestling with the shark and stabbing at it with the spear, she's grappling, climbing on top of it, letting

121

it swim on top of her, and now her costume is
unzipped right down and you can see

Why did Gerald bring me here it's not fair it's not
fair

I can't stop watching and I can't sit still and I've
drunk the rest of my lager in big fast gulps without
even knowing I was drinking it and my prick feels
like a firework with the fuse lit just about to ex-
plode just about to go off bang bang BANG BANG
BANG

The scene's over, they're going off, I'm going too,
I'm not going to stay here to be treated like this, to
be humiliated, to have everything spoilt for me, all
right if he wants to claim he's won, let him, he's
won, I wasn't strong enough.

I'm standing up. He's looking at me, but without
surprise. Probably thinks I'm going for a leak. Yes,
he's telling me:

'It's down that flight of stairs.'

I'm nodding, I'm walking away from the table.
No need to have a row with him, so I might as well
do it this way. If I told him I was getting out of here,
he'd raise hell, he'd point out that I don't speak the
language, I don't know the way home, I haven't
any money.

All that's true but so what?

The hat-check girl. I point to my coat and say '*Por
favor*'. She looks a bit surprised and a bit sullen, I
suppose most people tip her, but I can't help it,
sorry, dear, just give me my coat, give it to me and

let me get out of here before that girl shows me her tits again because sure as fate if she does I'll jump over the table and throw myself at her and I've got to be alone, I've got to be out in the cool dark street, I've got to be by myself in the dark and the quiet.

Down these stairs. Out of this door.

Clare, Clare, I couldn't help it. Are you still there, still near me somewhere, or have you disappeared, have you left me to myself now that you've seen what I'm like? I wouldn't blame you, I'd leave myself alone, if I could. It was too strong for me, Clare, I never knew till now. Right up to that moment I thought I could win.

What moment? The moment when I knew that I could hate something, despise it, see it as evil and disgusting, and yet *want* it, with a want, a need, a desire so strong that I knew in that second that it would win against anything, sweep aside anything, trample and splinter and smash *anything*.

Clare saw inside my mind, that's why she's gone into silence and darkness and why this long blank street is without her. I can't hide anything from her, and I know she was looking into my mind at the moment when the awful thought formed itself, so suddenly and so clearly:

the moment when I had the thought
the moment when I had to accept the knowledge
the moment when the knowledge came kicking

123

and punching and smashing its way into my mind

broke a wall down, punched a window out, came in with a shower of bricks and plaster into the thought-house I've been building for seventeen years, building it and living in it and choosing furniture and pictures for it

the knowledge

that if it came to a choice

if it came to a straight choice, there that minute or anywhere at any minute

a straight choice between having the World Free Zone and having that girl, not just any girl but *that one*, getting her on to a bed and fucking her, giving it to her for all I was worth, if I had the choice between doing that and seeing the World Free Zone established, seeing it spread from country to country till in the end it was supreme over the whole earth, I wouldn't hesitate, I'd have the girl.

I'm walking along, thinking these thoughts, the houses on either side are tall and unlighted and I don't know where the hell I'm going, but it doesn't matter any more where I go with my body, Clare, because I've nowhere to go with my mind any more. I mean, you can only live your life for a thing like the World Free Zone if it's the most important thing of all, if you wouldn't swop it for anything, and now I know there's a stronger force in the world, and what's more I know it's something I can't feel any *liking* for, just this mad pitiless desire. I hated her, I hated everything about her, her long

124

face and her big wide eyes with no thought behind them, and most of all I hated her silly get-up and the whole way she came on, mixing up her sexual power with cruelty and killing. I hated that silly spear-gun strapped to her thigh, they're illegal as a matter of fact, did you know that, Clare? Illegal, that's a laugh, it only makes it more attractive, come on, join me in breaking the law, breaking the rules laid down by decent people who care about the life in the sea, let's go hunting and kill something, stain the clean salt water with blood, and when we've finished let's pull ourselves up on to a smooth rock and you can unzip my swimsuit and we'll lie there in the sun and fuck, fuck, fuck. That's what she was saying without using any words, and I understood her and went along with it, I wanted her so much it swept my whole being towards her in a torrent, a torrent of blood and saliva and sperm, that's what I am, that's what I'm made of, and now I know it and Clare knows it too.

There's a street lamp in front of me but it's blurred, misty, I think I'm crying and the reason I'm crying is because all in a few minutes I've lost the World Free Zone and I've lost Clare. She won't want anything to do with me now she's seen the horrible dark slavering mindless way I can look at a woman, not being put off by hating what she is and what she does, but in a grovelling way actually wanting her more because of that.

That must be why she's gone, why I'm not

getting any signals any more. I've dropped out of her wave-band. I'm just not the kind of person she'd want to communicate with, or perhaps she still wants to but just doesn't find it possible. I'm too low, too grovelling, not evolved enough. The only kind of female being I can communicate with is that bushy-haired whore with the strapped-on spear-gun.

Apart from that type, I'm alone.

Alone. That word brings me back. There's a cold wind blowing up this dark cavern of a street. Where the hell am I? Which way ought I to start walking? Even on the assumption that walking'll do me any good. That taxi-ride was a long, long one, now I look back on it. I must be way the hell over the other side of the city. What city? Where am I? Lisbon, yes, Lisbon, I know that, but what is Lisbon? Do I know one damn thing about it? Do I know one person who lives here, do I know the names of the main streets, the main public buildings, do I know whether it's safe to walk about at night? Is it crime-ridden, infested with gangs? What happens to people who get lost in Lisbon at one a.m. – do they just disappear? Found on a rubbish tip with their throats cut, pockets slit open to get at their wallet and money, not that there's anything in my wallet except a provisional driving licence and a photograph of Libby Greenslade on holiday in Cornwall, wonder why I kept that, did she mean something to me after all?

I'd like to see her come walking down this long empty street now, old Libby, giving that shy puzzled grin. Well, it's all the better for her that she's not going to come down this street, that she's safe and tucked up in bed at home. What force picked me up without warning from Kenningbury, Berkshire, and dropped me down here in the middle of the night?

God, what a way to die. Not trying to *do* anything, not trying to save someone else's life or lead a revolution or anything worth doing, just drifting about in the middle of Lisbon at night because a fat slob wanted a bit of company in a knock-shop.

Well, why did you leave the aforesaid slob? At least he'd have got you home.

Because of the girl. I left because if I'd gone on sitting there I'd have had to watch her again. I'm in more control out here. Whatever happens out here it won't be a storm that shakes me into little pieces from inside. That's the worst thing.

But it's already shaken you, you're already in little pieces, and now you're going to have your throat cut. Fool.

Get a grip on yourself. It may not be inevitable. Perhaps not everybody who walks about Lisbon at night has their throat cut. Come to that, why walk about? Get into some safe hole and just wait for daylight. Watch the sky, hour after hour, from some nook where you feel secure and unnoticed, watch it until a faint streak of grey comes into it, then the streak gets brighter, and brighter, and then the sun comes up ... ah, God, let me see the sun again, tomorrow's lovely sun shining on the town and the hills and the sea.

A safe nook, but where? Here's this long street, narrow, silent, blank doorways looking at me, or, even worse, dark entries where any number of thugs might be lurking. A few quick steps forward, the flash of a knife, and that's me finished, and the World Free Zone finished, and everything ... never mind about the World Free Zone, that's shot anyway, even if I live, I was forgetting.

Where can I hide?

Nowhere, obviously. There's nowhere. The only thing is to walk till I come to a big lighted street, the sort of main thoroughfare that's lit up right through the night, and hang about there till a policeman picks me up as a vagrant. I don't like the thought of being arrested, it may be a bit tough at first, but the cop's bound to see that I'm a foreigner, some harmless imbecile who thought he'd have a good time and ended up lost and frightened. And then perhaps I'll get away with nothing worse than a night in the cells. I wouldn't mind being in a nice safe cell now, this minute, as long as I knew it wasn't for ever.

I want to run. I want to break into a mad, full-speed run and keep running till I ...

Till I what? Finish up sobbing for breath, can't

run a step further, couldn't dodge anyone who came towards me.

This won't do. Take a grip on yourself. Stand *still* while you decide what to do. Calm, planned action. Five, six, seven, eight, nine, ten.

There seems to be rather more light in the sky over on *that* side. That may be the bit where the town's awake all night, where the street lights aren't turned off: blazing department-store windows perhaps, people about, traffic cops. It might be all right there. Can only try anyway. Start walking towards it.

Left, right, tread, tread, my feet make a hell of a noise. The street's so dark and so silent. If I'd got cheap shoes with plastic soles I'd walk more quietly, but of course my parents see to it that I get correct, expensive, all-leather shoes that are healthier for your feet, leather's porous, it lets your feet breathe. Kenningbury's the sort of place where most people, a high percentage, a random high-percentage sample, wear proper expensive all-leather shoes and then they have healthy feet. Finish up in a dark street in Lisbon with healthy feet and a cut throat. Your feet go on breathing in their porous leather shoes even after your throat's been cut.

That's it, keep thinking, a procession of ideas going through your mind, march, march, just like your feet marching along this street in the silence and the HOOH OH JUMP ASIDE QUICK THEY'RE HERE

IT'S THEM THEY'RE AFTER ME COMING OUT OF THAT
DARK DOORWAY my heart my heart it's pounding
I'm frightened I'm frightened but after all
   after all
      after all
         after all
            it's only
              a girl.

She's standing there staring at me and there's
nobody else with her nobody looking over her
shoulder she's just standing there and I must have
startled her when I went HOOH and jumped. I must
have jumped about ten feet but now I'm standing
still and she's standing still too, there on the
pavement, staring at me.

Hey, kid, I won't hurt you. It's all right. You just
startled me.

I give her a smile, kind of apologetic, and then
she smiles back. I can see her face clearly, there's a
lamp fixed up on the wall of the building behind
her. She's very young to be doing what she's
doing, my age or even a bit less, but I suppose they
start them young. Perhaps she's an amateur, a
beginner. Certainly it seems a funny district to
pick, with no one about.

But she's a whore all right. No other type would
be standing about in the street at this hour, and her
get-up. Punk, sort of, with very high-heeled boots.
Her hair's very short and very fluffy, just like a
canary's down and exactly the same colour,

absolutely staring yellow. It may be the natural colour or it may be out of a bottle, but it *looks* unnatural and I suppose that's the idea. Her eyelids are painted bright blue. Under it all she looks very, very young.

Now I've calmed down enough to get an impression of her as a *person* and the first thing that comes into my mind is, She looks a *nice* girl. She's got up in a way that's as unnatural, as artificial, as it possibly can be, to make her look like a toy, but under the funny canary-fluff her little oval face is her own, and it's a nice face. If I knew her back home she's the kind of girl I'd want to take to the sixth-form disco. To a school disco in Kenningbury, Berkshire!

I almost burst out laughing at the thought of it.

She's looking a bit puzzled, staring at me, she must be wondering why, if I don't want her services, I'm standing here gaping at her instead of walking on. The fact is, I'm just so glad to be in contact with another human being in the middle of all this darkness and loneliness and fear. But now the thought grabs me, She could tell me the way! She must know the town, she could start me walking in the right direction!

I'm looking straight into her face, opening my mouth, but what the hell's the Portuguese for 'I'm lost'? And if it comes to that, what's the name of the hotel? My mind's gone blank, absolutely blank.

'*Pedido*,' I say to her, '*perdito*. Lost.'

131

And I'm tapping my chest to show that it's me I mean, not someone else.

She suddenly comes out with a stream of Portuguese. Oh, my God, hold it, hold it, I'm not getting any of this.

At least I've remembered the name of the hotel. It's come flashing back like a beacon.

'Miramar,' I say to her. 'Hotel Miramar.'

Then another brainwave. As she rattles out a bit more Portuguese – and I can tell from her tone of voice that she's willing to be helpful, she's not telling me to drop dead or anything like that – I remember my habit of carrying about a pen and a few bits of scrap paper, an old envelope or something. I was never more thankful for that habit. Out comes the ball-point, out comes an envelope, and I'm holding them out towards her, indicating that I need directions.

'Carta,' I hear myself saying. 'Map, *por favor. Diagramo.*'

I wonder whether any of these words exist? If not, they're pretty useful inventions because she's got it, she's taking the pen and the envelope, and she's making swift lines, talking all the time. A long line and she says, '*É large.*' Then a curved one and she planes downwards with her free hand and says, '*Desce a rua.*' That must mean downhill, go down a slope. I'm getting it. Now she does two parallel lines fairly far apart, to indicate a main road, and then swerves her body to the right and says, '*Volta a directa.*' I'm getting it, man, I'm getting it, this is marvellous.

Then she makes a big blobby circle and says 'Hotel Miramar.'

I take the pen and the envelope back and thank her. I keep on saying '*Obrigado, obrigado,*' nodding my head and spreading my hands.

She's stepped back a bit and she's looking at me, and suddenly it all strikes her as funny, or perhaps it's just me that strikes her as funny, but anyway she's giggling.

I don't know what the joke is but I'm feeling pretty happy, pretty relieved, and I start laughing too. We're standing here, in the dead small hours, pitch dark, under this one street lamp, wind getting up, rain beginning to come down, and we're *laughing*.

As I move off I wonder, the thought coming in from nowhere, why she's chosen this spot to stand in. Surely there's no custom here? The street as deserted as this? But perhaps she knows something I don't. Perhaps there's a secret meeting at the local anarchist cell and they're due to break up in a few minutes' time and she'll get them going past.

Or perhaps she really is just a novice who doesn't know anything about the game. How can you tell? To look at her, you wouldn't think she was on the game at all, wouldn't think she'd ever heard of it.

And, moving away now, I suddenly see again her little hands holding my pen and my scrap paper. Little hands, with thin fingers, like a child's.

Well, she's started me off, all I've got to do now is walk, walk, walk, it must be a hell of a way but that doesn't matter, I'm not tired, and what's more important I'm not frightened of walking at night any more. Somehow the little canary-girl has lifted that fear from me. So, I'm off on the long trail, but wait a minute, straight away, barely fifty yards from where she's standing, I'm at a standstill already.

It's one of those points where a number of streets – five, in this case – come together in an open space, a kind of circus though not masked by anything as formal as a roundabout. Do I go straight across, diametrically, or do I take a line slightly to the left or right? Standing here, on the edge of the round, lighted empty space, there are at least three that look about equally convincing. Stuck already! I turn and look back, oh, there she is, watching to see that I get this one right, and when she sees me look back she signs to me to go straight ahead, take the middle one opposite. I'm waving to her, thanks, thanks, good luck, I'll remember you, and I turn back the way I was going and plunge on, over the intersection, on to the street that leads the way I have to go, and suddenly you're there, Clare, I know you're close by me.

Sixth report to Clare

Now I'm not alone. We're going along together. I'm walking and you're, sort of, *floating*, well, not quite that, you're keeping the rhythm of my footsteps. Anyway, you're coming along with me. Funny, it's as if that wave I gave the girl, a wave that just tried to send my thanks and friendliness to her along fifty yards of dark empty pavement, also acted to bring you to my side. Why did you come just at this moment? I think I know; I think it was because I'd pushed down the barrier I was beginning to build up between me and your sex, your gender. I'd had some good and loving vibrations towards another feminine being.

And now I walk on, thinking, my mind full of one big question. Clare, what is it to be feminine? What is a woman? Is there a woman-ness, a femaleness, that they share and that sets them apart from maleness? I've sometimes heard people talk as if there is, and I've read things that seem to have the same idea, like that Lawrence book they pushed down our throats in sixth form English. But if there is a femaleness, a woman-essence, what is it? Is there something in common between

(a) you,

(b) the girl I've just been talking to, with her fluffy yellow hair and her thin little claws and her childish little punk-face: so far, pretty easy, I could put the two of you in something like the same box with no trouble at all, in fact, and I know you'll understand when I say this, she reminded me very much of you in some ways. But when I get on to

(c) the girl in the cabaret, the one who drove me mad, with her long upper lip and big empty eyes and that horrible spear-gun strapped to her thigh, and on past her to

(d) Mother,

I really start running into trouble.

Can you help me, Clare? I'm listening to anything you want to tell me. And if not now, walking along this street, then any time you like. And if not in words, then communicate it any way you like. If you have some knowledge to give me, feed it directly into my blood and bones and my nervous system.

The spear-gun girl, even: if I could think of her as a *person*, I might not feel her as nothing else but a hot, steamy channel of concentrated sex – but no, I can't manage that yet, I'm not ready for it. When I think back on *her*, I become nothing but a colossal erection walking down a dark street.

Well, walk on, walk on.

I'm tired. My legs are aching. I feel like sitting

down propped against a wall, drawing my knees up, resting my leg muscles. But I'm going on, and I'm getting somewhere. This street's wider, and better lit, than the last one. Ahead I can see light rising up into the sky. I'm getting to some central part of the town, where it'll be safe to walk. I'm not worried about that any more, for some funny reason, but still it'll be good to get to where I can relax and just plod on.

Streets, streets. This city's very foreign. It was built by foreign people, and they're all round me, sleeping, waking, all having foreign dreams and foreign thoughts. What does it mean, to be foreign? How different does it make you feel? To them, I'm foreign. What would they think of the World Free Zone, if a few of us really did come here one day and try to set it up, with our yellow huts and all the rest of it? Would they be glad to see us, glad about our ideas, wanting to join us and make it a real success? Or would they be suspicious, not wanting us? Would they make up lies about us and spread hate-ideas until one night a crowd of them with clubs and gleaming torches came trampling into our little area?

What area? There isn't going to be any area. The whole thing was just a dream, and not a dream I'm all that sorry to be rid of, either.

I'm learning a lot in the course of this one night, and I seem to be learning it in stages. First I realised I wasn't the kind of person who *could* preside over a

World Free Zone, and now it's sinking in that the World Free Zone isn't the kind of thing that needs presiding over anyway.

Clare, are you listening?

How many years have I been day-dreaming about the World Free Zone? Two, Three? It seems to have been for ever. Just dreaming about myself being somebody important. Our Founder. The World Free Zone owes its existence to that man of vision and statesmanship, blah blah. I see it now, walking slow and tired along this empty street; if I can sit with a few friends and share thoughts in trust and respect, we shall have the World Free Zone there and then, without formally setting it up.

Look, I dreamed up all that stuff because I hated life at our house. Not because it was in Kenningbury, Berkshire, not because it was our house, but because of my parents. And the particular thing about my parents that made me hate living with them was their marriage. Right from the start I saw one thing clearly about the W.F.Z. – it would have *no marriage*. Why, all I was doing was just to try to find a way out of my own mess – or rather, their mess that they'd wished on me.

Suddenly it doesn't matter any more. I mean, I can live with them without letting their mess get *inside my mind*. I can be my own person.

And besides, Clare, they're not so bad. God,

when you put them beside somebody like Gerald. If I've had them on my back, what would it have been like for that poor little sod Charlie, if he'd lived?

Clare, don't go away. We're nearly home. I recognise this street. It's the ten-lane one! There's the building with the big red walls and the funny turrets! The hotel! It really exists, it's there!

Seven

My last fear, pounding along this final stretch of pavement – will the hotel be open? Is there a night-bell you can ring? Do you have to make arrangements if you're going to be in after about one o'clock? Why, *why* did I just stalk out into the night without going up to see them and tell them what I was doing?

I didn't *know* what I was doing. Just going out with Gerald.

Well, that would have been enough. They'd have mentioned that the two of you might be late. But you didn't want to, you were independent, didn't want to ask them for anything, you were a big man, you were going out to see the world and grow up in one evening. Well, you made a mess of it, didn't you?

Sod you. Clare understands.

Funny, the two halves of my nature still arguing even now that I'm half-running, half-stumbling the last few yards. The hotel lobby looks lit up, but dimly. The sort of lights they leave burning when a place is closed, just to keep burglars off. I'm nearly there, I'm there, I'm taking hold of the door handle, it opens, yes, I'm inside, there's a night porter, that stooped old bloke with his green uniform and brass buttons that need polishing, or perhaps they're just old, tarnished. Like him. But I love him. I love everything about the hotel. It's home, and my own language, and sleep, and safety, and, yes, it's my parents.

That thought came from somewhere in inner space. My parents? I went out to get away from them. I couldn't stand another night under the same roof as their tensions and quarrels, my mother's drinking, my father's black moods. I went out. The big world. Lights, music. And above all don't let Them know where you're going. Let them wonder, let them worry if they want to, let them get it into their heads that you're free, you're independent of them now and for ever. Only, it doesn't feel like that any more. That's just a feeling I *remember*.

The key to my room isn't here. Someone's taken the key to my room, it's gone. Hey, old tarnished man. He's grinning, toothless, explaining something. Not a word of English. Something about, *Chave*. Something about, *No quarto*. That must be the room. The key's in the room.

He's let my key out of his possession, that's what he's done. I could have him sacked for that, though of course I wouldn't dream of having him sacked, I love him too much. Perhaps I left the key in the door. I was excited enough to make a silly mistake like that. I go up the stairs, one flight, two flights.

All round me, people asleep in their boxes of sorrow. Wrapped in sheets of sadness, resting their heads on bladders of tears. Their children gone. Black bleeding holes where their children were pulled out of their chests. Asleep, wandering among nightmares of flames and gravestones. Asleep, or lying awake in the grieving dark. And my two? Clare was pulled out of their chests. What will they do about the holes? One may try to fill the hole with whisky, the other with absences, departures, meaningless offstage adventures. Or could I do anything? Am I any good at hole-filling?

I'm going to my room, though I have no key. If it's locked and I can't get in, I'll go down and get a skeleton key from the old man. But perhaps it'll be open. And it'll do me good, make me feel safer, just to walk down that corridor, with my parents asleep behind one door and my own little one-night box of space at the end, with my toothbrush and pyjamas waiting in there.

Here's my room. There's a vertical line of light: the door's ajar. Push it open a few inches; peer in. It's her. My mother. She's sitting in the chair by the bed. She looks across at me, tired, but quite wide awake. Sober, awake, waiting for me. *Waiting?* For *me*?

Sit down on the bed. Springs jog softly. Wait for her to speak first.

'Hello.'

'Hello, Mother.'

No more. Is she going to stay silent? Is she hard, angry? No, she's smiling. An exploring little smile, but not challenging, not taking any kind of war into my country.

'Did you have a good time?'

'Not specially.'

Nothing's going to make me talk about all that, nothing. Push the subject away. Ask her what she's been doing.

'Have you been waiting up for me? I hope you weren't worried.'

It sounds a silly question, how stupid to be polite in that rather tea-party way when such enormous things have been happening, but I honestly can't think of anything else to say. I want to reach out to her but I just don't know how to. I also feel foolish to be standing there, in the middle of the room, while she sits in the armchair by the wardrobe, but there isn't another chair.

So she sits, and I stand, and I look across at her. My mother. All through the years of childhood she's been just an extension of my identity, I've thought *my mother* as I might have thought *my foot* or *my stomach*, and all this time she's been a real separate person, living her own life, or at least living some kind of life and calling it hers. And now she's sitting there, in this cramped, rather meaningless little room where she's been waiting for me God knows how many hours. Have I ever seen this woman before? Her face looks tired and lined in the overhead light. The room has two lamps, one in the ceiling and one at the bedside, but the bedside one is a little fringed toy of a thing that only makes a circle of light, it doesn't reach across the room to her. It's the overhead light that strikes down and makes her dark-red hair look heavy and greasy, which it isn't, and her face pouchy, which it probably is but needn't be really. Standing there, staring at her, I suddenly see her whole life as being like an arrangement of lamps. Her husband, my father, gives off a fairly strong light that ought to be enough to perceive things by, but it strikes *down*, flattening everything under it. And I'm too small-scale, too weak, too much of a little toy lamp with a fringed shade, to reach across to her and make any difference.

She's always been quite important to me, because after all my foot's important, or my stomach, but now all at once I see her differently, and I know that she's important to me *as herself*. What I mean is, and I force myself to make room for the thought as it settles into my mind, what I mean is that I love her.

She's looking at me now, almost as if thinking that it's her turn to do some staring, almost as if wondering who I am.

I must sit down. I go over to the bed and sink on to it. No, I must *lie* down. I keel over, slowly, and come to rest on my back, with my head on the cool pillow. Oh. God, that feels good. Oh, it's delicious,

delicious. My aching bones sink into the softness of the bed, my fluttering muscles can soften and let go. This bed receives me like a mother, and I love it, but still I don't love it as much as I love my real mother. I turn my head to one side and look across at her.

She's wearing the grey dress she wore for the requiem service; of course, she'd have no reason to change, and as I look at her sitting straight in her chair it strikes me that the dress is well chosen for her colouring and well cut. She's got style. How does a person with style end up with such an unhappy life?

I say again, because I want to reach out to her, want to say I'm sorry for any extra pain I caused through being bloody-minded:

'I do hope you weren't worried.'

She looks at me with a dead expression, drained of all feeling, like a person who's put all emotion behind her, who knows she'll never feel strongly about anything again.

'No. I thought you'd probably come home.'

Before I can stop myself I say: 'But you waited up for me.'

I didn't mean to say that, I didn't mean to make so much of it, to sound so eager. I meant to play it cool about her waiting up for me, the way she's playing it herself.

'Your father was worried.'

I hate the way she says *your father*, the way he

145

might be described by a stranger, by a hotel servant
or a policeman or something. She goes on.

'I waited up for you because that was the only
way I could get him to go to bed. Correction, I
couldn't get him to go to bed at all. All I managed to
do was to get him to take his shoes off, and his
jacket and tie, and lie down on the bed. And that
wasn't till about three o'clock.'

'What was he doing?'

'Fussing.'

I suppose I ought to be content with that answer,
it's fairly obviously intended to stop me pushing on
any further, but I can't help it, I have to know.
Lying there with the soft welcome of the bed
reaching up through my body, I admit it to myself;
it matters to me how my father and my mother feel
towards me because it matters to me how I feel
towards them.

'Can you tell me any more than just that? Just
that he was fussing?'

She turns that blank face towards me, it's almost
like the utterly expressionless faces you find on
some sea-creatures.

'He was quite sure something dire had happened
to you. He kept buttonholing the manager and
asking him to telephone the police and say you'd
gone missing. The manager quite obviously didn't
want to, he was bored with the whole thing and he
wanted to go to bed, and anyway I don't think he
wanted to pester the police and get on the wrong

side of them. He wrote out the Portuguese for "I want to make enquiries about a missing person," and Ben had that piece of paper in his hand and was downstairs for hours, working his way round all the police stations and hospitals. Fawkes was helping him, some of the time, and then he got fed up too, and went off to bed.'

I pictured it.

'Could he understand what they said to him at the other end?'

'No. I think he just got passed from one strange voice to another, none of them saying anything he could understand. The manager wouldn't let him have the use of the office telephone, so he had to use the one in the foyer and he kept running out of coins. He had the hotel porter scouring the whole of Lisbon to get him a supply of coins, going into all-night cafés and God knows what.'

I couldn't stand it, I could see my father's drawn, tense face, I could hear his voice repeating his one magic phrase over and over again, hoping there was somebody out there who could give him information about his son. He'd lost his daughter and now his son had walked out into the foreign night and not even said he was going.

Somebody at the other end ought to have said, Your son's sitting in a night-club with a glass of expensive lager in front of him, staring at a babe in underwater gear with a spear-gun in her hand and her tits bobbing about, that's where he is.

I feel terrible. I say to my mother:

'He must have been pretty upset. Were you down there with him?'

She looks at me in that dead, incurious way, as if it were a question that concerns two other people.

'For part of the time, yes. Finally I gave up and came up here, tried to read. I even fell asleep for a bit, and when I woke he was still down there, feeding coins into the damned box. I decided to put my foot down then, I told him it was just getting too silly and either you were coming back or you weren't, but trying to telephone wouldn't affect it one way or the other. He didn't want to come, but I practically dragged him up here and made him lie down. Even then he'd only do it if I said I'd go and sit in your room, so that I could go and tell him straight away if you came back.'

'Did he go to sleep then?'

'He said he wasn't going to, that he was only lying down to keep me quiet and he'd get up again soon, but within a couple of minutes of lying flat he was dead asleep. He was so all-in.'

'Will you go and tell him I'm back now?'

'No. I shan't wake him.'

I say, carefully:

'It's a good thing you insisted on him lying down. He might have cracked up altogether, with one thing coming on top of another.'

'Yes. I told him he wasn't going to get any sympathy from me if he drove himself over the edge.'

She says it in this toneless, metallic way, but suddenly I don't want to believe it, I can't bear to believe it, and I say quickly:

'That's not true, is it?'

'What's not true?'

'That he wouldn't get any sympathy.'

She says nothing. Her hands are folded in her lap. I go on.

'You can't mean that the only reason you don't want him waking up is because you don't want the nuisance of having to nurse him.'

She says, as if talking to herself:

'There was a time when I wouldn't have minded nursing him. There was a time when I wouldn't have minded doing anything for him.'

'There was a time, but that was then and this is now, is that what you mean, Mother?'

'I don't know. I think so.'

She pauses, then talks on faster.

'A couple of years after we got married, he went to a conference somewhere a long way off; really a long way, Indonesia I think it was. He was there two or three weeks and he used to send me air-letters. I can remember the first one I got, I stood there in the kitchen holding it in my hand and I thought, what an incredible distance this has travelled, from Ben's hand to mine. Across seas, across mountain ranges, across deserts, across people speaking all sorts of different languages. I felt . . . awed, somehow. And now we stand in the kitchen and look at one another and the words we speak have to travel just as far.'

Suddenly, I'm thinking of Clare. She ought to be able to help, especially now that she's got so much power.

I'm trying to come up with some words that will bring Clare into the conversation, but while I'm fumbling for them it seems as if the thought of her has travelled across the room without words, because Mother starts talking on a new tack, one that's going to bring Clare in.

'One thing that's always been clear and solid about Ben is his fondness for you two. He had doubts about wanting to be a husband, but he was always very glad he was a father. I remember once when he'd been away on a trip. Abroad somewhere. When he got back, I met him at the station and I had you two along with me – I had no one to leave you with and I used to take you everywhere with me. You were about, oh, six and two, I suppose. No less than that, five and eighteen months; Clare wasn't walking properly yet, I held her on one hip as we stood on the platform watching the train come in, and you were dancing up and down beside me holding my other hand. Ben was hanging out of the window to get his first glimpse of us. He told me afterwards that he had a very rapid double-take. When he first saw us, his mind registered, what beautiful children! And right away, in the same fraction of a second, it registered, those are *my* children! After being away from you for a week or so, it was your beauty he saw first.'

I'm sitting up now, to listen better, and I ask her: 'Why do you remember that now? Why does it come to your mind?'

She pauses.

'Because he talked about it last night.'

'Last night?'

'In the middle of all that hooh-hah about telephoning, he came up here to get some more money or something, and I made him sit down and we rallied a bit.'

'I'm glad you did that.'

'It wasn't difficult. To get him to talk, I mean. As long as one stayed with the only subject he was interested in talking about.'

'What was that?'

She gives me a level look that I can't quite read.

'You and Clare, of course. He's very churned up and all sorts of things are surfacing from deep down in his mind, things he probably hasn't thought of for years. He just talked in an uninterrupted stream for about half an hour and then suddenly jumped up and said he must go down and get on with telephoning. Didn't wait to hear if *I* had anything to say. But I forgive him for that. Perhaps if I'm a good listener for a bit, he'll listen when it's my turn to talk. Not that I've got anything much to say. There's nothing bubbling up from the bottom layer of *my* mind – it's just like a frozen pond.'

'I'm sorry. I'm sorry it's like that.'

'Oh, ice is quite useful stuff. You can walk on it. People don't get drowned through ice unless they walk on it when it's on the point of melting. That's the only time it's dangerous and I have the feeling that's the only time I'd be dangerous. Well, to go on about Ben. He rambled on about how beautiful you both were as young children, your perfectly shaped little limbs and bright eyes and oh, all the rest of it.'

She passes her hand over her eyes as if suddenly she's under great strain. I just keep quiet and she goes on.

'I had the feeling there was something else coming – that what he was saying was sort of the first half of what he was trying to get out, and I wasn't wrong. After he'd finished rhapsodising about how wonderful it was to have you two as little angels, he got on to what it was like *now*, with Clare gone and you so much changed.'

'Oh?'

'Yes. He said it was really the thing that was driving him into a panic about you. He said if anything awful really *had* happened and you didn't come back, if he never saw you alive again, he wouldn't be able to endure living with the thought of what your face had been like the last time you looked at him. When he asked you if you'd go out with him and you just said you wouldn't, you must have made up your mind already that you were going to do something else but you didn't tell him anything about it. You just said no and looked at him with your face absolutely closed. That's what he said. He said your eyes were like two stones.'

My father. I gave him two stones.

'He kept saying he had to find you and get you back for his own sake. If he had to go through the rest of his life seeing your face as it was then, he'd have to kill himself.'

I can't sit up any more, I'm keeling over again, now I'm lying on my back staring upwards, but the light's too bright, the overhead light is bringing tears to my eyes, or at any rate something is, the bulb looks all blurred and I can feel the hot rivulets on my cheeks, and now I'm turning on my side so I'm not staring up at the light any more, but the tears go on. Quite silently, but thickly. I just lie there, on my side, with my back towards my mother, and they're rolling down. Perhaps I really am crying, really crying about something, but it doesn't matter what, just let it happen, let it happen.

The bed bounces softly. My mother has come over and she's sitting beside me. Then, just as she used to do when I was little and I couldn't sleep, she puts her hand on my head and starts moving it through my hair. It's like the wind moving quietly through long grass.

She's talking again and her voice is gentle now.

'I understood what he was saying. I feel it myself. People talk as if kids need their parents, but after the first few years, it's the other way round. I said that to Ben and he said, "That's true. They're stronger than we are. We're lost and they've got a home." I asked him how he made that out and he said, "Looking at them from the outside they seem to wander about and we seem to stay still. But actually it's the other way round. We're waifs and they've got somewhere to live. They live in the future. It's a very strong place to live because it's fortified with hopes and dreams. By the time people get to where we are, they've no hopes left; only a few dreams and they're fading."'

Her hand moves away from my head and she stands up.

I'm warm. That's the thought that comes to me as she moves very quietly over to the door and out, closing it gently behind her. It's the thought that always came as a little kid, when she'd been to see me in bed if I was ill or frightened or upset. I'd call her and she come up to see me, she'd always come. She could make any bad thing go away, she could tame the shadows in the corners of the room, and she could make my head go back to its normal size when it seemed to have swollen out into a great monstrous globe. She'd stroke my head and calm me and then when she went I'd be left feeling only

one thing, the warmth of the bed. I'm warm, I'd say
to myself, I'm warm, and before I'd said it more
than three or four times, I was asleep.

I'm warm, now, just like that, and yet I know I'm
not a little kid. I'm not sinking into any kind of
dream that's making me regress, or whatever they
call it. I know I'm me, Paul Waterford, seventeen, a
sixth-former, and what else? Founder-to-be of the
World Free Zone? I don't know, because once I
think of the W.F.Z., I think of that girl in the
nightclub, the one who blew it all sky-high. I can
see her long upper lip and Cupid's bow and her big
eyes and her round scarlet nipples. She's looking at
me and she's smiling, so, *laughing*. She's finding it
funny that she's proved to me that I can't manage,
can't cope, can't stay on top. She's glad because it's
confirmed her in the things she does, it's proved
that her world is the strongest after all. I didn't
know sex could break my will like a straw. I didn't
know there was *anything* that could do that, and
now I know she can do it, a long-legged bushy-
haired girl in a rubber bathing dress, unzipped
down the middle, and a spear-gun strapped to one
thigh. That's all it took and I was finished. Finished
as the boss, the Supremo, the authority-figure who
had his values all in their right places and put first
things first.

Perhaps, as I lie here warm and relaxed, so glad
to be safe, so glad of my mother's love that still
lingers in the air of the room, perhaps, the thought

comes, there are still things I could do. She took that spear-gun off her thigh and shot me, I know that, I felt the spear going in and my hot blood running out, I know I'm a wounded person. No wonder they show Cupid with a bow and arrow. When I looked at her in that slowly changing light, yellow to blue to red to green, and her nipples always dark and her hair always shining, it was just as if something was going right through me – an arrow, or her blasted underwater spear, or just a red-hot poker of lust, but *something* that was going to leave me, for the rest of my life, wounded. So what? Can't a wounded person do things?

Yes, but not things like that. Not things that involve supporting other people where they're really weak, in their hidden souls. Not things that involve guiding people towards truth and peace.

You say that. But who the hell are you? Just Paul Waterford, just a kid who hadn't grown up enough to know what temptation was, what the strength of it could be. Well, now you've learnt something. Pick yourself up and start again.

Start again, yes, but from where?

I'll tell you. From humility. If that babe with her underwater act wounded you, destroyed your belief that you were in control, then all right, *be* a wounded person, look with eyes of compassion and equality at other wounded people who still manage to push their lives along, still manage to give something to the world. Your drunken mother. Your indecisive, absentee father who can't get his talents together. Everybody in the world is wounded, start from there.

Start from there. But for the moment, before you even start, be warm; lie here in this soft bed, letting your legs go slack and the tiredness drain out of them; feel the gentleness of your mother's hand on your forehead, feel the gladness of knowing that you love her, that you see her quite clearly as a human being who makes mistakes, who sometimes even makes herself ridiculous, who has her failures and weaknesses, but how good it is, how strong and deep and comforting, to know that you love her, you love her.

Seventh and concluding report
to Clare from
Kenningbury, Berkshire

Home. Up the stairs, hello house, hello banisters, the view out of the windows. My room. Bed, all-purpose table, bookshelves, record-player, tape-recorder, all the usual junk. That globe they bought me when I was about twelve, a great big coloured ball of possibilities, it's still dominating its corner of the room near the window. (I wonder if living with that globe gave me the idea of the World Free Zone? Made me want to fence a bit of it off and have my own way there?)

My room looks exactly as it did yesterday morning. And yet different. Nothing's changed, nothing's been touched, and yet I see it differently after making my longest journey, so far, away from it and back. My longest journey. You can say that again. Quite a trip.

Hello, kid. Thanks for being here. I didn't really doubt you would be, you're such a part of everything that's going on, I knew you'd want to be with us and share in it all – and surely if you want to be, you can be. But of course I couldn't be completely certain till I got home. Now I know you're here, not just around generally but here, in my room.

So I'll sit down a bit and we'll talk. I mean, I know you must have been there and seen everything that's happened, but on the other hand I feel it'll help me to catch up with it if I tell you the story from my angle. Things have been going so fast, both everything outside me and everything inside me has been just roaring along, I want to sit down quietly, here in my own room among my own things, and spell it all out to you.

It seems strange, looking at the spring afternoon still bright outside the windows, no sign yet of the light starting to fade, to think that this morning, *this* actual morning, I woke up in that little hotel room in Lisbon. I'm not used to travelling, I suppose, but on the other hand I hope I never do get used to it, I enjoy the feeling that I've been transported by magic from one place to another absolutely different, and all in the same day. Makes me feel what a lot of room a day has in it, if you just use it right. So I woke up in Lisbon, and at first I didn't know where I was. Then I remembered, and remembered as well that we had to be ready not long after nine, to get out to the airport. I looked at my watch and it was after eight already, my God! I threw the bedclothes back and sat up, and it was only then that last night came flooding back to me. I washed and dressed quickly, with the thought going through my head that the first thing to do was find out what state the parents were in. I'd given them a pretty rough time and they might have fallen into an exhausted sleep, in which case it would be my fault if they missed the 'plane home, and enough things had been my fault already. So I got ready double-quick and went along and knocked at their door.

I had to knock good and hard for a long time before it opened. There stood the old man, in his clothes except for jacket, tie and shoes. He must have keeled over on the bed like that, just as Mother said. He'd just dragged himself out of deep sleep, his face was crumpled and toad-like with big shadows round the eyes. But he smiled when he saw it was me, and his whole face seemed to get into a firmer shape and even to become a bit less grey.

'Hello, Paul,' he said.

'Hello,' I said. 'I thought I ought to give you a call. Is Mother up?' And I tried to see past him, into the room.

'Better come in,' he said. 'She's not only up, she's gone out for a walk.'

'A walk?' I looked at the piece of paper he handed me. In Mother's big, clear hand was written:

Ben, you're sleeping, I'm glad. Paul's back. I feel very wide awake and the dawn's beginning to come up, so

I'm going out for a walk. Didn't see anything of the city yesterday and they tell me it's very beautiful. Get good rest. M.

'That's nice,' I said. To myself I thought it might have been nicer yet, but it was nice enough to be going on with.

He nodded, and grimaced again, and walked into the bathroom, I heard the shower splashing away and then he came out towelling himself.

'Better get on with it,' he said. 'Mum can join us at breakfast.'

'Aren't you going to ask me where I was last night?' I said.

'No,' he said, pulling on a shirt. 'You went out without telling me where you were going to and I know you'll tell me when you're ready. For the moment, all that matters is that you're back safely. And we haven't got much time to talk, compared with what we'll have later on.'

Well, I had to admit that made pretty good sense. I wasn't too keen on talking about last night, anyway. It was all a bit recent – my mind hadn't settled down yet.

'Besides,' the old man went on, doing up his shoes, 'I want to get down there and find out what they're going to do about Mrs Finlayson.'

'Do about Mrs Finlayson? What's the matter with her?'

'She's gone off her head. She came howling into

161

the lobby while I was trying to telephone the police in the early hours of this morning.'

'Howling? Mum didn't tell me about that.'

'She didn't know. She couldn't hear it from up here and I didn't bother her with it.'

Then he told me what had happened. At about one-thirty in the morning, he and Fawkes had been downstairs, using the hotel telephone. At least Fawkes, who knew a few phrases in Portuguese, was taking his turn ringing round the police stations. Not because he wanted to, but because Dad had got him more or less by the scruff of the neck and made him do it. They were standing there, Fawkes holding the telephone and Dad right behind him, willing him on, when Mrs Finlayson came dashing down the stairs in her nightgown. Mr Finlayson was two steps behind her with an overcoat that he was trying to get her to put on, but she was in too much of a hurry. She wanted to speak to Fawkes. It seems she'd woken up in a very rigid state, not shouting and screaming, just very determined and with her mind fixed on one simple idea. I don't know whether you know about this, Clare – probably not, unless in your new state you've got some kind of gift of splitting yourself into more than one consciousness, because round about that time you were over on the other side of town keeping an eye on me.

Her idea, Mrs Finlayson's, was that the 'plane crash had been a judgment on the parents for wickedness. She didn't think they'd *all* been wicked, but regarded as a group they had been, and that's why their children had been taken from them. It seems the notion had been building up in her mind ever since the trip started out – even before, perhaps. I suppose she just couldn't grasp the awful thing that had happened, couldn't get to terms with it, and this was how her mind solved the problem without actually disintegrating.

Anyway, Dad told me, she stood there in the hotel lobby, with her husband behind her trying to put the overcoat over her shoulders and generally clucking. She took no notice and started in on Fawkes – quietly at first but raising her voice till at the end she was pretty well yelling. The minister, that's what she called the parson, the minister must come back and do his stuff over again. What he'd done and said in the church service had been all for nothing, he'd missed his chance. Now she wanted him brought back to go through the whole thing again in the hotel breakfast-room or somewhere. It could all be fitted in before the flight home, she was quite reasonable about it, nobody was going to miss the 'plane or have their arrangements thrown out, only they must be told they were sinners and their children had been taken up to heaven as a judgment on their wickedness.

'The minister must come back!' she kept saying. 'You've got a telephone there, speak to him now! Wake him up! He must come here at dawn and the people must be woken to hear of God's judgment on them!'

Dad said Fawkes had simply not known what to do. It was no good just telling her to calm down; on the other hand if she went on like that she'd wake the whole place and then the management would probably insist on having her sent to the local nuthouse.

'What was your reaction to it all?' I asked him.

'Oh, me. I hardly noticed her. To me she was an interruption. You see, I wanted Fawkes to get on with the job of establishing contact with the police and anything that came between me and that objective was just an intrusion. I'd have felt the same about an earthquake.' He said all that quite matter-of-factly and added in the same tone, 'Are you ready to go down to breakfast?'

'Yes,' I said. It was about the longest speech I felt capable of making, at that moment.

We walked along the corridor and down the stairs and he finished telling me about Mrs Finlayson. There wasn't much more to add, actually. Fawkes had undertaken to ring up the clergyman, just to humour her and get her to go back to bed. Fortunately, she didn't stand over him to see if he did it. And then he'd gone into the hotel kitchen and mixed her a hot drink and put some kind of Mickey Finn into it, to knock her out. It must have been quite a busy night for him.

I was still turning over all this in my mind as we

sat down at the breakfast table and got started on orange juice and eggs and coffee. They don't seem to have heard of toast, but there were little hard rolls that did nearly as well. We were just making a start when I happened to glance across at the doorway and saw Mother standing there, looking round for us. She had on the light tweed overcoat she'd worn for the journey yesterday and her face looked fresh and relaxed. My immediate impression was that she looked good. She saw us and came over, very springy and self-possessed. There was something guarded in the way the old man looked up at her.

The table was laid for four so there was an empty chair, and she put her coat over this and sat down.

'Good walk?' he asked her.

'Marvellous,' she said. 'The city looked so beautiful as the light came up. Those houses with tiles all down the front – they were glistening. I'm so glad I saw it.'

Then she looked at him as if amused to see him tucking into breakfast, after all the agonies that had happened. 'You woke up in time, then,' she said.

'Paul woke me, or I'd have been sleeping now.'

'Well,' she said, 'that's as it should be, considering Paul was the reason you got so little sleep.'

Here we go, I thought. I kept my eyes down.

'Don't let's talk about it,' the old man urged. 'There's no point in dragging it up.'

'Why not? I think it's a very natural thing to talk

165

about.'

Now, I thought, they're going to give me hell. Well, I suppose I deserve it.

'Paul didn't do anything wrong,' she said, in a voice that was calm, but, what shall I say, *challenging* at the same time. As if she were determined to bomb him out of a prepared position.

'Didn't do anything *wrong*? Going off without—'

'That's just it. He went off by himself without saying where he was going or even that he was going at all. In other words, he just felt he had to cut off communication with us, freeze the whole dialogue and get away by himself, pretend for a few hours that we don't exist. Can you honestly say you blame him?'

He tapped his cleaned-out eggshell as if testing its thickness. After a pause, he said, 'No, I can't.'

'Nor can I,' she said in that calm, precise voice. 'We must be pretty desperate to live with.'

I tell you, Clare, I really started wondering what the hell was going to happen next. I mean, she seemed so *strong*. As if she was ready for anything, even to have an inquest on their married life right there and then, over the eggshells and crumbs.

'Are we, Paul?' the old man turned to me. 'Are we hell to live with?'

I wanted to say, Yes, you're hell, but I'd rather have you than Gerald. But of course, I didn't. They wouldn't have known what I was talking about. So I just looked from one to the other of them and said

166

nothing.

'I suppose we must be,' he said to her. 'The kind of pressures we build up. It must get too much to bear, for anyone having to share our living space.'

'Yes,' she said.

'But then,' he said, as if thinking aloud, 'it might be possible for us to do something about it.'

'Something about what?'

'Everything,' he said, and as he spoke he looked up at her and I think he looked straight into her eyes, 'Everything,' he said again.

She leaned back a little in her chair and said, 'You mean if it'll help Paul to stay in line?'

'Paul's important,' he said, 'but Paul's one thing and we're another. There's a lot we can improve whether it makes any difference to Paul or not.'

'I think so too,' she said, as if he had said something like, It looks likely to rain before lunch-time. Then she said, 'What's the time? We ought to be getting ready, oughtn't we?'

'We ought,' he said, 'but you haven't had any breakfast. Where the hell's the waiter?'

'Never mind breakfast,' she said. 'Just a swallow of coffee. This'll do me if you can spare it.' And she took his cup, which was still half full. There was a clean cup beside her plate and she should have poured the coffee into it, but she chose to drink out of his cup. I thought that was a good sign.

We all got up to go and just at that moment Fawkes came in. He paused as he came past our table and Dad asked him. 'How is she?'

'In sedation, naturally,' Fawkes said. 'What she'll be like when she wakes is anybody's guess. The . . . fit may have passed. Or she may be worse. All we can do is leave the husband to cope. And I've laid on a doctor. He'll be in attendance when she comes round.'

Just then, Mr Finlayson appeared in the doorway. I thought he must be coming in to breakfast, but he just looked in, not as if he was searching for something but just straight ahead, as if his eyes weren't seeing anything, and then he went away.

'He'll be the next to crack up,' Fawkes said gloomily.

But Dad shook his head. 'No. He can't afford to crack up. He'll stay on his feet and function, till his wife recovers.'

'And then?'

'And then anything could happen.'

'What are you talking about?' Mother asked.

They told her.

'There's one thing you don't seem to have thought of trying,' she said. 'It might put her right more quickly than sedation.'

'And what's that?' Fawkes wanted to know.

'Go along with it. Do what she wants. It wouldn't have done any harm to have the clergyman come back and go over it all again, and this time allow for the possibility that she's right.'

'Right?'

'Perhaps we have all been wicked,' she said in this rather cheerful, businesslike way.

'If we have,' Fawkes said slowly, 'that's not why the children were killed.'

'We don't know that,' she said. 'We don't know anything.'

'True enough.'

'So the parson might just as well have come back and spoken to us all at seven o'clock this morning.'

'He wouldn't have come.'

'If he wouldn't,' she said, putting down her empty cup, 'so much the worse for him.'

We all sat there for a moment longer, thinking about this, and then Fawkes said, 'Well, I must help to organise us off. See you on the 'plane.' And he went out. It struck me, looking at his back moving away, that he, as well as the old man, had kept off the subject of me going off and causing them all such a lot of trouble.

That reminded me. Where was Gerald?

I felt a bit guilty about him, all of a sudden. I'd left him pretty high and dry, when he'd been looking forward to a bit of company, even mine. On the other hand, I wasn't afraid that he'd come to any actual *harm*, not in that plushy place. If I'd left him in the first joint we went to, I could just have imagined him sitting there getting more and more drunk until finally he slumped and got robbed. Or murdered, even. But in that second

169

place, they had more subtle ways of fleecing people without bothering to go through their pockets.

Then three or four people got up and went, and I saw that Gerald had been there all along, sitting in a hidden corner, out of everybody's way. He was drinking a big cup of coffee and, as far as I could see, not eating anything. His face looked pale and puffy and his eyes were like pools of piss in the snow. But he saw me looking at him and gave a little wave, and a half-grin, with something like his usual jauntiness. Good old Gerald. At least he keeps his little flag flying, even if it does need laundering.

Then there was the clumping up and down stairs with suitcases and what-not, and the nagging to get ready, and the hotel manager standing about giving everybody a big smile which was really just his relief at getting us all off his back. The coach was nearly due. I looked round at the crowd, sitting around anywhere they could find a place to sit or standing guard over their luggage. As my eyes picked out one face after another, I found myself wondering whether they looked any different, whether this last twenty-four hours had changed them at all. But then, did I look any different? And a hell of a lot had changed for me. The World Free Zone, for instance, was going to be buried in a grave near the seashore at Lisbon. Somewhere near where I'd admired that nice motor-boat and thought of how I could go exploring in her, and find a place to set up a colony. Well, all that had blown away. It just didn't belong in my mind any more. The things the World Free Zone had been *for*, they still mattered, but that wasn't the way to go about them.

The foyer was busy and cluttered and I was sitting down on my suitcase pretty well screened by the plant with the big rubbery leaves, as when Mother and Dad came down I saw them and they didn't see me. I looked at them good and hard. There was something *different* about them. I tried to pin it down, Clare, so that I could tell you about it, but I couldn't and I still can't. The nearest I can get is to say that they seemed to be moving like two people who are going somewhere together instead of just walking in the same direction by accident.

So the bus came and we all fussed around while the luggage was put into a trailer to be towed behind and all the rest of it. I didn't remember any of that palaver when the same bus, or one exactly like it, was bringing us in from the airport, yesterday, instead of taking us out. It's as if people were giving more thought to their possessions and their normal routines, now that the mourning was officially over, as if they were saying, today's a *normal* day.

As we all moved towards the bus in a packed, shuffling mass, I was a few paces behind Them, and I noticed one little detail. As they stepped up on to the platform of the bus, he touched her elbow lightly – she didn't need any help, it was just a gesture – and she very lightly swayed her body towards him, as a woman might do in dancing.

So, who's to say whether it meant anything or not? But I noticed it.

Now I was standing there, my feet on the ribbed floor of the bus, holding on to one of the metal uprights, and Lisbon was flooding along outside the windows, the same Lisbon as yesterday, but in reverse, like a film being re-run backwards.

I wonder if I'll ever see the place again. And as the bus swooped along I wondered, too, what the little girl I'd met in the doorway was doing at that moment. She wouldn't be still in the doorway, of course; she'd be catching up with her sleep. Alone, probably. I wondered if she had had any customers in what was left of the night, after she'd put me on the right road. But my imagination switched off at that point; I couldn't picture her serving a client and I don't want to.

Gerald was on the bus, right down the other end, but I could only see his shoulders and the back of his head because he'd managed to grab one of the few seats. Didn't feel up to standing, I suppose.

The last stretch of coast road, with those palm trees and the blocks of flats and the garages and filling-stations and then it was Lisbon Airport, everybody out, and we were herded into the terminal building. All present and correct, except the Finlaysons. Funny, that it should be one of *them* who cracked up. They seemed at the beginning to have the lid screwed down so firmly on everything. That must be why.

They rushed us through the last few minutes, passport formalities and all that, at colossal speed. It was as if, now that everybody had done what was expected of them, they couldn't get rid of us fast enough. Standing there, waiting to be called out on to the tarmac to board the 'plane, I found myself for some idiotic reason thinking about school. I pictured the History sixth at Kenningbury Comprehensive, halfway through the first period with old Horton rambling away about the Settlement of 1688 or something like that. The way Horton goes on about 1688, you'd think it had Settled everything for ever. I think the end of the seventeenth century must be his dream country, the way the World Free Zone used to be for me, only safely in the past. Well, to each his own.

Are you still with me, Clare? Sorry, I got a bit wrapped up in my thoughts then, a bit dreamy, forgot I was trying to make it all clear to *you* as a way of making it clear to myself. The fact is, I didn't get enough sleep last night. Makes me a bit dreamy. Everything had that mad logic that you accept quite naturally when you're dreaming.

The stewardess told us to start moving and we all went out on to the tarmac. In the general milling, I was separated from the parents, and it happened that I was just behind Mr and Mrs Smithson. We were all carrying flight-bags and raincoats, and we were headed off and streamed about like a flock of sheep being moved along by dogs. We had to walk about three hundred yards to where the 'plane was waiting, away from the terminal building and then past some long, grey featureless hangars. As we walked, something about the man Smithson attracted my attention. He seemed not to be looking where he was going. His long stalk of a neck was fully extended and his head was slowly turning from side to side, like the beam of a lighthouse. I almost expected to see it make a full circle and to find myself looking into his eyes. His wife had noticed something, too, and she was taking his arm as if to lead him along if he was determined not to look where he was going. Then, suddenly, he stopped dead.

Those of us who were behind him stopped too, for a second, and then started to flow around him on either side as the water of a stream flows round a rock.

Clare, were you there? Did you see what happened?

His wife was pulling gently at him, trying to get him to go on, and I heard her say, 'We'll be on the 'plane in a minute,' in a sort of pleading tone, as if trying to tell him that all this terrible Lisbon experience would be over then, that they could sit back in their aircraft seats and begin to get themselves together and go back to normal life. But he took no notice, he just stood there for another few seconds and then he said, 'Wait here. I've seen Tracy.'

'You've *what*?' she wailed. 'Oh, Jim!'

Jim was deaf to whatever she was conveying. He moved off down the long, narrow space between two hangars. People had begun to notice, now, that something was amiss, they were stopping and pointing him out to one another. He walked away, with those big high blank walls on either side of him, like a solitary figure you'd see in a dream.

Then he called 'Tracy! Tra-a-acy!' It was like a dog howling.

The parents had got as far as where I was now and Fawkes was with them. We all stood together, looking at him as he walked further away. Mrs Smithson was crying. Mother put an arm round her shoulders and began saying things to her, things I didn't catch.

Fawkes looked all-in. Enough had happened to him in the last twenty-four hours; he was pretty tough and capable with it, but he couldn't take any more.

One of the other parents said, 'We'll just have to leave him. Airport security'll pick him up, anyway. They won't have him just wandering about, getting on the runways and everywhere and causing accidents.'

Fawkes looked round a bit wildly, as if searching for something to focus his eyes on. It was our old man who spoke.

'We can't leave him. We can't just get on the 'plane and go and leave him behind. If the airport police arrest him they're probably not going to do it any too gently. They're not gentle types. He doesn't speak the language and if he has to spend a night or two in the cells, or come to that in a mental ward, it could throw him off what remains of his balance altogether.'

Good thinking, I said to myself. I didn't know the old man had it in him. But I'd seen nothing yet.

Smithson had got to the far end of the space between the hangars. One of the stewardesses ran after him, caught up with him and tried to take his arm. It was a mistake to touch him. He didn't seem to know she was there until he felt her hand on his sleeve. Then he whirled round in a sudden convulsive movement. I don't know whether he meant to hit her, but he did. He caught her across the cheek with the back of his hand and she staggered back and then put her hands over her face.

The stewardess was one of our own that we'd brought along. I found myself feeling glad it wasn't a Portuguese citizen that he'd hit. I had visions of hard-faced policemen with big boots and fists, giving him a bad time.

Dad must have had the same thought, too, because he turned to Fawkes and said, 'Wait for us. I'm going to get him on to the 'plane.'

Fawkes said simply, 'How?'

'By whatever means it takes.'

And the old man walked away from us, towards the corner of the hangars where Smithson had now disappeared. Just at that moment a 'plane that was standing right beside us started up its engines and we were all engulfed in that impossibly loud screaming noise. Nobody could hear anyone else, we could only communicate by waving our arms and such-like. In the middle of all this one of the aircraft personnel, a man this time, the Purser or something like that, came along and started to herd us all on. They wanted those of us who were still sane, at any rate, to get on board and stop causing problems. Mrs Smithson didn't want to go. She stood still and clung to Mother and so Mother had to stand still too. I could see her mouth moving as she tried to say things to Mrs Smithson but of course nobody could hear anything. I started to move along, and as I did so the aircraft engines went silent for a moment, and I could hear Mother saying to the man from the aircraft:

'She wants to stay and see what's going to happen about her husband. You can't make her get on the aeroplane while she still doesn't know if he's coming or not. You must see that.'

He said, 'My instructions are —' and then the jet-scream started up again and drowned everything.

The Purser, or whoever he was, stood there looking as if he couldn't decide what to do. I didn't

blame him. But I hadn't much attention to spare for
him because I was staring at the empty space at the
end of the two hangar walls. Somewhere out of
sight, round the back of one of those buildings, my
old man was walking towards a chap who had,
quite probably, gone off his head. My mind flashed
back over all the times I'd seen Smithson since this
trip began, and I remembered the rigid way he held
his body, and the not-quite-human look in those
popping eyes with their unreal china-blue colour. It
seemed to me, looking back, that he had been a
madman from the start. Just the sort of madman
who commits crimes. Including murder.

I could tell Mother was thinking the same kind of
thoughts. Her face was very pale within its
surround of dark-red hair. Her jaw-line was very
tight, as if she had her teeth firmly set together, to
bear whatever was coming next, and she stood
very straight.

The aircraft stopped its engines again and the
only sound was Mrs Smithson crying, a soft,
snuffling background noise. She sounded like a
child of about three who's got over the loud wailing
stage of crying and settled down to a sort of fretful
nobody-loves-me snivelling. She held on to Mother
as if afraid that if Mother went, the universe itself
would go and leave her spinning for ever into a
black hole. I didn't blame her. I knew just how she
felt.

Where was Dad? Would we soon be walking

round the end of that hangar and finding him lying
on the ground, strangled by Smithson or with his
brains beaten out? I started to run forward. The
Purser shouted something at me, I think, but I just
ran on. I came to the end of the space between the
buildings and looked right, then left. Nothing, I
turned left because I thought that was the way I'd
seen them go, and started to run again. When I got
to the far corner of the hangar I stopped. In front of
me was a big open space, the main airfield, and
parked out on the runway was the 'plane we were
due to go home in. Walking away from me,
towards it, were Smithson and the old man. They
were only a few yards in front and I saw them very
clearly. Smithson was walking stiffly, as if he had
to make a separate decision every time he bent a
knee or straightened it. He reminded me of a
clumsily made working model of a tall wading-
bird. The old man was keeping step with him and
had his hand inside Smithson's crooked elbow. I
could hear his voice, though I couldn't make out
any words. He was talking to Smithson in a low,
comforting voice, taking him on step by step
towards the 'plane.

I walked back to where the women were
standing. It was all over. My father had coped.
Smithson's wife could take him home and begin
very slowly to put him together again, and herself
too; I could see it would take a long time. Certainly
she would have to begin with herself – she was

right down, no strength left.

Walking towards them, in the thin morning sunshine that lit everything up and picked out every detail, the lines of expression in people's faces and the folds of their clothes, I had a sudden feeling of hallucination. It may have been something to do with not having had enough sleep, plus the emotional state I was thrown in by all the things that were happening so fast – but whatever it was, I looked at Mrs Smithson's face as she stood there clinging to my mother, and I saw it as the face of a young girl. And at the same time, somewhere just behind it, I saw the face of the little canary-blonde, the teenage whore in the doorway. Had *she*, that young girl who must have been a dozen or fifteen years younger than Smithson's wife, had she, at any time since leaving her childhood, crumpled like that? Had she needed help and support, begged openly for it, cried out for it, like the woman I was looking at? And if so, who was it she had turned to?

I saw her thin little face through the white, anxious face of Mrs Smithson, and God knows I wasn't making light of what the Smithson woman was going through. If I had been making that mistake, my mother's face would have been enough by itself to put me right; it was so grave, so tender, so strong. She was *giving* to this poor weak little woman, giving, giving, and that pouring out of her strength was keeping her own anxiety from swamping her.

But the little whore! The little canary! She must have been through some time of being desperate, some time when life showed her a face just as hard as the face it was showing to Mrs Smithson now. Because it must be true that a girl doesn't go on the streets without terrible pressure from *somewhere*. She doesn't just wake up one day and decide that it'd be a nice career to stand around in a doorway and get screwed by all and sundry. Either that or just stand there for nothing, with the rain coming through her shoes and the wind blowing through her jacket. Surely she doesn't get down *that* low without some weight pressing down hard enough to break her?

And if she had cried out, if she had clung, who had been there? Anyone? Or just emptiness?

The hallucination went away and I was looking in normal daylight at poor little Mrs Smithson, crying, clinging to my mother. And the Purser, standing there next to them in his white shirt and peaked cap, with the little bits of gold braid on his shoulders looking somehow silly, as if they underlined his helplessness.

I had important news for all of them, I was the centre of things; I swaggered.

'It's all right to get on board,' I said. 'Dad's got him under control.'

Mrs Smithson didn't seem to hear me, she went on crying, but Mother closed her eyes for an instant as if a silent prayer of thanksgiving had swept through her body, and the Purser said, 'Where are they?'

'Going towards the aircraft,' I said, 'look,' and at that moment the two of them came into view on the far side of the hangar, Smithson still doing his crane-walk, Dad still keeping that calm grip on his elbow.

The Purser turned and hurried away towards the 'plane. The three of us followed, more slowly. Mrs Smithson had dropped her flight bag on the ground. I picked it up and carried it for her. She had stopped crying by now. Mother was saying, 'You'll be able to get him to bed when you get home, and if I were you, I'd get in beside him. What you both need is to sleep for a week.'

As we approached, Dad was helping Smithson up the stairs into the rear entrance, with the Purser following on as if ready to catch the pair of them if they fell backwards. Then they were all inside, and we were the last, and airport workers in clean overalls were waiting to move the ladder away. We went up, Mrs Smithson first, Mother next, then me. I was the last of our party to stand on Portuguese soil. It gave me a slight, meaningless feeling of distinction. I felt as if I was rolling up a carpet that all of us had been walking on for twenty-four hours.

Twenty-four hours? Was that all?

Inside the aircraft, most people were sitting

down. I looked down the length of the cabin and saw that our row of seats, the ones we'd had coming out, were empty. I supposed we would move down and get into them. But Dad was standing beside the seat he'd put Smithson into.

'I'll sit with him during the flight,' he said to us. 'We don't want him suddenly thinking he can see his little girl walking on the wing or something.' Then he said to Mother, dropping the slightly jokey tone, 'Thanks for waiting out there.'

'They tried to make me get on the 'plane without you,' she said. 'But I wouldn't.'

'I knew. I couldn't see you but I knew you were still out there.'

'How did you know?' she asked him.

He gave a little shrug. 'Everything feels different when you're not there. It didn't feel different so I knew you were.'

I couldn't see her face, because I was behind her, but as she looked at him I saw the look that came into his face.

We moved on down to the front and sat in our seats, with an empty one between us. Take-off. Portuguese ground falling away. Roads, lines of toy cars, houses of Portuguese shape, would I ever see them again?

Whether or not, we droned on. Now and then I took a look at Mother. She was sitting back very comfortably in her seat, not reading, not sleeping, just sitting there looking very calm. What action

183

there was, was going on deep inside her.

When I went back to go to the wash-room, the old man was sitting next to Smithson. Smithson was asleep, or at any rate his eyes were closed. His wife was snuggling up against him with her head on his shoulder, as if she was already anticipating Mum's advice about getting into bed with him. Dad gave me a friendly smile as I went past. Had he *forgotten* that I'd crucified him with worry all night, or had that part of the whole experience just got lumped together with the other parts, and had the total come out as something positive?

Back in my seat, I just sat there and watched the clouds. They were shaped into enormous tufts, like icebergs, or towers in a fairy-tale. The 'plane moved through a clear sky that was as blue as water, and on each side, and above and below, there stood these great motionless shapes, white as cotton wool. It was much more like submarine cruising than flying, as if we were nosing through some enormous coral reef in the sky. A far cry from that phoney underwater scene in the nightclub.

When they came round to ask if anybody would like a drink from the bar, I was going to have a glass of lager, but I changed my mind at the last moment and had tonic water. Mother had a whisky, but she took a long time to finish it and she didn't get out her flask.

Then it was fasten seat belts, London, we were coming down, we were down, and it was picking up overcoats and flight-bags and shuffling down the aisle and getting out into the cold fresh breeze on the tarmac. Dad came up to us.

'You two can get yourselves home, can't you?'

'Yes, but what are you going to do?'

'I'm going to drive the Smithsons. Their car's here but she doesn't drive and he isn't in a fit state to. I'll come on home by train as soon as I've got them there.'

'Where do they live?' I put in.

'Near Southampton somewhere.'

Mother said, 'What on earth train will you get from *there*?'

'There's bound to be a service of some kind. I'll find out and ring you up when I know.'

'Don't worry,' she said. 'You're doing the right thing and we'll meet you from the station whatever time it is. Or would you like Paul to come with you, to co-drive?'

'Not worth it,' he said. 'We'd have to put L-plates on their car and anyway I'll feel happier if Paul's looking after you.'

So we agreed on that.

Then it was a flurry, goodbyes here and goodbyes there, suddenly the whole group was washing away like a clod of earth thrown into a river. In the middle of it I ran into old Gerald. He looked at me as if he thought he'd seen me before somewhere, but couldn't quite place me.

'Hello,' I said.

185

'Hello, Paul,' he said. So he had remembered who I was. 'Get home all right?' So he had remembered what had happened.

'Yes, thanks,' I said. 'It was a bit of a walk, though. Sorry I cut out a bit early.'

'You missed the best part of the evening,' he said.

There didn't seem to be anything to say to that, so I just gave him a grin and left him.

Mother and I waited for our cases and when they came bumping up through the heavy plastic flaps, I knew the trip was finally over. Quite a trip though.

As I carried our cases towards the exit I caught a glimpse of Fawkes. A decent man. But very much in the past, now. I felt you telling me that, Clare. It was the first message I had from you after landing in England. *Ironstone is over*, you said, didn't you? As if, from now on, the things that happened to you and the places you went to are in the past, though you're in the present, always.

We went up in the lift to where the car was. Walking towards it I was surprised, somehow, to see the L-plates. Still a learner, after everything that had happened in those twenty-four hours! Learning to get into dialogue with you, Clare, and learning to live without the World Free Zone hanging up there in the future like a lighted sign in the sky!

Why didn't you tell me that was all nonsense, Clare, when you must have known? Letting me find out for myself, I suppose. To think it only took one chick romping about in a coloured spotlight wearing a rubber bathing dress.

Ah, well.

I was just stowing the suitcases into the car – we'd taken Dad's, too – when Mrs Richardson walked past, without seeing us, on the way to pick up her own car. The car she'd shared with her husband, who was a scatter of ashes now in the sea-breeze in Lisbon.

I started up and took us down floor after floor, then off through a tangle of streets, shops, bus stops. As we went along we chatted, easily, like very old friends. When we got to the motorway, I was quite willing to go on driving and risk it, but Mother said she'd take over.

'Imagine,' she said, 'if we were stopped by a policeman and had to spend hours at a police station being questioned, and then we weren't at home when Ben rang up.'

'We wouldn't have to go to a police station at all,' I told her. 'They'd just take our names.' But I let her have her way. And she let me take over again when we left the motorway.

Altogether, she seemed pretty cheerful and relaxed. It was as if the trip had done her good, settled her emotions. When we got home and let ourselves into the house, she went round all the rooms, as women nearly always seem to do when they get home after an absence, instinctively marking out their territory. Then she got us a snack kind of lunch, some soup and scrambled eggs, and while she was getting it ready, I sat in the kitchen and chatted and kept her company.

She hadn't had a drink on the 'plane, and it was about half-past one when we got to the house, so I wasn't surprised when she got a bottle of whisky out. It was a new one. She twisted the screw top off and broke the little metal ring round the neck. Then she poured herself a stiff one, drank it quickly, and filled the glass half full again.

I didn't say anything. It wasn't my business.

We chatted some more and ate our lunch, and I was just wondering what to do with the afternoon, whether to stay with Mother or leave her alone to get drunk and sleep it off, when the telephone rang. You won't need telling, Clare, that it's on the kitchen wall, so all Mother had to do was get up from her chair and answer it. Straight away I could tell, just from listening to her side of the dialogue, that it was Dad ringing up to say when he'd be back.

I tried to hear what he was saying but I couldn't. She asked how he'd got on and how Smithson was. He talked for a couple of minutes non-stop and I could only guess the kind of thing he was saying, but at the end she said, in a kind of bantering way, 'You seem to be making quite a success of your new career, old thing.'

What career? he must have asked.

'People putter-together,' she said. 'Picker-up of

life's casualties and sticker of them back into one piece.'

I wondered if she was taking the mickey out of him, and if so whether she was doing it kindly or intending to play rough. I couldn't tell from her tone, and her back was towards me so I couldn't see her face.

He said something or other that must have been a joke, and she laughed. It was a nice laugh. Accepting, sharing, not mocking.

Then she took down the arrival time of his train and said goodbye and hung up. But what I noticed when she turned round was that her face had a contented look, as if something was making her feel that things might work out all right. I don't want to overplay it, you understand, and in any case, I realise that you know more about it than I do because I expect you can look into their minds. I'm just telling you what it looked like to me.

She asked me if I'd like a cup of after-lunch coffee and I said yes. She made two cups and I noticed she didn't finish the second shot of whisky. Just left it standing there.

After lunch she said she'd go upstairs and rest for a bit, which was understandable enough considering how little she'd slept the night before and that she'd been walking round *Lisbon*, for God's sake, at first light on this very day. Lisbon! Is it in the same galaxy as Kenningbury, Berkshire? I suppose it must be because we all went there and came back and we're the same people. Well, nearly the same.

I told Mother I'd wash up and she agreed to let me. When she'd gone upstairs I gathered the dishes up and of course, there was her whisky glass, still with most of the stuff in it. I hesitated a moment and then washed it down the sink. She could always pour some more out of the bottle if she really needed it when she woke up. But I wouldn't put temptation in her way by leaving a half-finished glass just asking to be finished for tidiness' sake.

So that's it, Clare, that's where we've got to now. She's still asleep and it's beginning to get dark. I shall go to the shop and get some food, just anything basic that we seem to be short of, so that when Dad gets home, which won't be long now, he can have a meal. I'll keep everything going all right. And if Mother doesn't wake up by herself I shan't wake her. I'll drive the car down to the station by myself and to hell with the law. I think she needs to sleep. She may, she just *may*, be sleeping herself into a new life.

It would be nice, wouldn't it, if the World Free Zone turned out to be something you could make without actually *doing* anything, just by altering the inside of your mind?

Eight

It's dark now. Mother's still asleep. I suppose we've been home about five hours, but the time hasn't dragged, it's gone by more like a dream. I went and bought the food and then I just sat about. I turned the television on but there wasn't anything I wanted to see, picked up a book but couldn't keep my mind on it, and in the end just put some music on, quietly, and sat and half-listened.

I'm still doing that and now the telephone's suddenly ringing out in the shadowy house and I'm hurrying towards it, clicking lights on as I go.

Peep-peep-peep-peep-peep. Call-box.

'Dad here.'

'Are you at the station?'

'Yes. Any chance of being picked up?'

'Not a chance, a certainty. Be with you in five minutes.'

I've hung up and now I'm going upstairs, peering in at the bedroom door, and she's still asleep. Out to the wide world, but not drunk, I swear. It's more like suspended animation, the whole organism slowed-down and pausing. Somewhere inside her there's a chrysalis and when she wakes up it's going to emerge as a new butterfly.

I'm waiting for those butterfly-wings and so is Clare. I can feel her, waiting and looking forward.

The car-keys, the car, I'm a learner-driver going on the road without a licence-holder sitting next to me, too bad, the station's only five minutes away and I get on fine.

I'm turning into the approach road to the station, deserted on a cold spring night, and he's there, with his flight bag and his mackintosh and his soft tweed cap. Coming up to the car as I stop and get out.

'Where's Martha?'

'She's asleep. I didn't want to wake her. How did you get on?'

He grins, and suddenly looks tired.

'The Smithsons are at home and they're going to be all right. But it's been a long day.'

I'm opening the passenger door for him, talking him in, soothing him.

'The long day's over now. Come on, I'll drive you home.'

He settles in.

'You broke the law, coming down by yourself.'

'Tell me something I don't know. I didn't think you'd want to walk home.'

'I wouldn't. Thanks.'

I start the engine and engage gear. The headlights cut a half-circle out of the darkness as we turn round and head for home.

Quite a trip.

Q4